Shelter

at

Sugar Beach

W. M. ANDREWS

CR&O

Sparrow Ink
www.sparrowink.com

ISBN - 978-1-989634-64-6

www.wendymayandrews.com

Stay in touch with Wendy May Andrews and all her upcoming publishing news.

Sign up for her biweekly newsletter at wendymayandrews.com

She's determined to avoid romance and happily ever after. Life has other plans...

Veterinarian Tina Archer is grumpy and proud. Being widowed young from a terrible marriage can do that to a person. But she's been living life to the fullest and isn't a bit sorry.

Until a routine medical exam reveals the toll her freedom-loving lifestyle—and the stress that comes with being a single mom—has taken on her health.

She knows it's time for a life makeover and she'll do what needs to be done.

But when her son's Big Brother program matches him with the annoyingly charming Clark, everything gets *really* complicated. Because how is she supposed to handle a man who seems so eager to knock down all the walls she's built around her heart?

All Tina knows for sure is that it'll take a lot of soul searching—and help from her friends—to figure out if a second chance at love is worth the potential cost.

She can only hope Clark will still be around when she sorts it (and herself) out...

Shelter at Sugar Beach *is an angsty but wholesome and delightful Contemporary Women's Fiction novel. Readers of all ages and backgrounds will love the empowering message at its heart.*

This women's friendship fiction book will bring you all the feels. If you love women's fiction with a side of clean romance, this is a great fit for you.

Dedication

Dr. Tina is a handful, especially at the
beginning of this story. Women can often gain
a certain reputation when all they're trying to
do is take care of business. That can make one
a little cranky. I know. So this book is for all
those who know what they want and plan to
get it but don't want to be thought of as a
meanie while they do it. I see you and love you

XO

Acknowledgements

My first acknowledgment has to go to my awesome, supportive husband. Without his easy-going nature and technical assistance, my books would never make it to publication.

My beta team – Monique, Alfred, Suzanne, and Christina – are the first to ever lay their eyes on each book and give me invaluable feedback. Your assistance is always appreciated, thanks for being on my team!

Editors are every author's most important partners and I am blessed with two – Bev Katz Rosenbaum and Julie Sherwood. If you find any mistakes in this book, those are entirely the author's fault.

My gorgeous cover is thanks to Les at GermanCreative.

Chapter One

The mirror did not accurately reflect Tina's state of mind, that's for sure, she thought as she regarded herself critically. She had done exceptionally well with her makeup and hair. Anyone looking at her might be excused for thinking she was happy for her friends.

"You *are* happy for them, you idiot," she whispered to her reflection. "They're your friends and if they want to get hitched, you're going to smile and nod and clap or whatever the guests at a wedding are supposed to do. And you're going to be happy for them, whatever the outcome. Because they're your friends."

Perhaps if she kept repeating it to herself, she would start to believe it.

But it wasn't Rachel or Jake's fault that her life was a dumpster fire and had been for the last dozen years. No one, especially not today's bride and groom, had forced her into getting married at such a foolishly young age. And it was her idiot former husband who had chosen to walk out on her and their unborn baby only to die suddenly in a car accident after leaving her with seemingly irreparable self-esteem issues.

No one knew that, and no one was ever going to know that. As far as her sweet, little boy was concerned, his father had been thrilled about his impending arrival and it was the greatest tragedy that he hadn't survived to see Tyler's birth.

Tina might be all dark and twisty, but she had no intention of putting that on her son. She did her very best to shower him with love, affection, and attention, even when it didn't come naturally to her. It was for that reason she was even willing to consider signing her son up for the Big Brother program his school was organizing.

The thought of allowing him to go off with a stranger made her want to throw up even more than the thought of attending her friends' wedding that afternoon, so she tried to push it from her mind. One problem at a time was more than enough, she reminded herself as she tried to do some of the affirmations and breathing exercises Rachel was always espousing. The fact that Rachel wasn't a woo-woo tree-hugger-type was the only reason Tina would even consider trying such a thing. Rachel swore by her breathing and sayings. While Tina had zero confidence they would do her any good, they weren't likely to hurt her either. And she needed all the help she could get that afternoon. The very fact that Rachel and Jake were her friends was part of why this was going to be so hard for her.

Tina was anti-marriage. There was no other way to put it.

She tried to hide her feelings from everyone since she had no intention of ever explaining why she felt so strongly. And it wasn't as though she was pro shacking up or anything like that. She was basically of the opinion that adults should be fully autonomous. Of course, that might curtail any population growth, she thought with a twisted smile as her gaze strayed once more to the paper on her dresser.

With a stifled oath, Tina turned the paper over. She couldn't deal with all the things at once.

She wanted Rachel and Jake to be happy. And they seemed fully convinced that marriage was going to make them even happier than they already seemed to be, so Tina was trying very hard to support the foolishness. She would do her best not to say anything disparaging out loud. And she would also make a concerted effort not to throw up while she was at it.

But oh the things she was thinking about their rash decision to wed would curl their hair.

Deep breath in, hold for four, out for four, in for four, out for four. With a whoosh of air, Tina let all the air out in the count of probably one, she thought with another wry twist of her lips.

In both theory and in practice, Tina believed strongly in honesty. For the most part, anyway. It was really only on the subject of marriage, her own to be specific, that she would lie to your face and smile while doing so. No one need ever know how perfectly disastrous her marriage had been. And the fact that Tyler had resulted from said marriage just went to prove that it wasn't truly a complete disaster.

But marriage was not for her. And she was struggling to wish her friends well. But well she did wish them. Honestly, she did. In the months since Rachel had moved back to Cape Avalon, Tina had learned to accept her friendship, and she truly tried not to be the unpleasant creature she had become.

It was a wonder she was having any success with her clinic with how barbed and cranky she could be. She didn't mean to be such a vitriolic mess, but it often happened without her conscious thought. If you asked Tina to describe herself, she honestly wouldn't use such negative words as rancorous, catty, or hostile, but from the things she heard around town, those were certainly words other people used for her.

She supposed it was only the merest coincidence that had made her a success – the fact that no other vets had tried to set up shop on the small island – and she should be grateful not bitter. But gratitude was far from her forte.

That was another thing Rachel had done her best to convince her about ever since Tina's recent doctor's visit that raised so many red flags. She had been fortunate that doctor-patient confidentiality had prevented the clinic from sending the results to the insurance company when Tina realized there was no way their good rate was going to go through after those tests. She would stick with her current insurer until she could get the health concerns under control. All her results had been "borderline" – borderline high blood pressure, borderline pre-diabetic, borderline high cholesterol, borderline lung capacity. Tina was beginning to hate the word borderline. But according to Rachel, the breathing exercises and affirmations were going to help. Tina was also supposed to be keeping a gratitude journal. She wasn't very good about writing it down, but she was starting to fall asleep at night to the cadence of her thoughts about what she was grateful for that day. Tina was determined to count that as a win since she had been struggling with sleep issues ever since Tyler was born. Even though she wasn't yet keeping good track of what she was happy about in her life, getting some sleep could only be a good thing. Even if it was a woo-woo idea, she would take it, almost like an adult version of a bedtime story.

That thought finally managed to bring a smile to her face, which was what she had been waiting for. Despite her feelings about Rachel and Jake committing themselves for life to one another, she needed to be able to smile at them that day, no matter her convoluted thoughts on the matter.

As she took one last look in the mirror and frowned over the pounds she had just started working on getting rid of, Tina shook her hair over her shoulders and shrugged. It was their life, they were fully grown adults who happened to think the mistake they were making was the most brilliant decision possible. She didn't have very many friends. She was determined to be supportive of the few she had. Even if that meant smiling at their wedding. Tina would support them that day to the best of her ability and on into the future, whatever that might bring.

It was a short drive to Rachel's house. They had decided to have their small ceremony on the beach in front of it. Some would probably think it romantic. Tina thought it was messy.

Of course, it wasn't messy, she argued with herself. That side of the island was where all the people with too much time on their hands lived. The beach was always tidy and groomed within an inch of its life. It was just the thought of getting sand into her pretty sandals or all over her new dress that was making her sceptical of the location. But since Rachel was pretty much alone in the world and even Jake didn't have a big family, they decided to keep all their arrangements very small. And they had romantic notions about declaring their eternal love on the exact spot where they had realized they truly loved each other.

If Tina didn't ridicule it in her own mind, she'd probably puke from nerves on their behalf. What was going to happen when the new wore off? What if Jake changed his mind and decided to leave Rachel? While Tina didn't think Jake was the sort who would ever lift a finger against a woman, she hadn't expected that sort of behavior from her own husband, either. Where would poor Rachel be then if he turned into a different person unexpectedly? She had already faced so many tragedies in her life.

Tina started the box breathing again. She wasn't going to be of any support to her friends if she had a breakdown on their front porch.

You've got this. You're smart, you're strong, you're calm, you're in control. Other people's decisions don't control you. You've got this. You're smart, you're strong, you're calm, you're in control. Big breath in, hold, deep breath out.

Rachel would have a good laugh at her expense if she knew what Tina had to do to get through her wedding day. On the other hand, she might be highly insulted. But Tina would ensure the other woman never found out. Even her few friends had no idea how dark her thoughts could get. And they would never find out, she swore to herself. No one could know. That was the only way to make sure Tyler never knew.

Tyler was the brightest spot of light in her entire life, and she was going to keep it that way if it took every drop of blood in her over-sized body.

Okay, game time, Tina. Happy, party face required, she whispered to herself as she stepped onto the beach carpet that had been installed for the special occasion. That was a nice touch, she acknowledged as she glanced down at her impractical but pretty shoes.

"Bride's side or groom's?"

"I beg your pardon?" Tina had been too busy concentrating on her feet to notice the guy standing at the back of the chairs.

"Which side are you? Team Rachel or Team Jake?"

Tina blinked again as though she couldn't understand what he was trying to say, but it was really to clear the shock from her vision. The guy in front of her asking such ridiculous questions was also the best-looking man she'd ever seen. Just her luck that he appeared to be the dumbest as well.

"I'd like to think I'm both their friends," she began. "Also, they weren't planning on being that formal, were they?"

The guy's rich chuckle did weird things to her stomach, making Tina frown, resulting in cutting his laughter short, for which she was slightly disappointed but tried to ignore the odd sensations.

"No, you're right," he said. "I'm just trying to meet people as they arrive. I'm new to the Cape, I just started working for Jake recently when he decided to cut back, but he was gracious enough to invite me to come along today." He ducked his head bashfully in a way that any female other than Tina would think was charming. "I guess my nerves made me awkward. I'm sorry."

Tina waved her hand in an attempt to be gracious. "Don't worry about it. Weddings can be awkward as all get out, you won't be the only one, I'm sure."

This prompted another deep chuckle, and Tina concentrated on not frowning in reaction.

"Let's say I'm Team Rachel just because I'll always take the girl's side if forced to choose, but I actually went to high school with both of them, so if it wouldn't cause a traffic jam, I should really have a seat in the aisle."

Tina felt pretty proud of herself for what she'd just said. It was borderline witty, if she did say so herself, making her seem both pleasant and approachable, not at all like her true self.

"That's cool," the handsome guy answered. Tina almost shook her head. She ought to have a tag for him other than handsome guy. She didn't want to be thinking in such terms about anyone. The only handsome guy in her life was Tyler. And he was nearly eleven and not even present that day. "So, you probably know everyone here, then."

Tina let her gaze bounce around the already gathered guests. He was right. "I do, actually. But I grew up here and only left temporarily for college and such. So, it is to be expected, I suppose. Rachel didn't plan on many or even any of her old colleagues from Chicago to come to the wedding, and I've met Jake's relatives from away who might be coming."

"So, you could introduce me around," the handsome guy said eagerly, prompting a return of Tina's frown. She added to it by stepping back and shaking her head.

"Sorry, dude, you're on your own. That is not a look I want to sport today."

Dude appeared puzzled but Tina refused to explain herself, merely turning on her heel and marching away. Thankfully, when she'd scanned the gathering, she'd spotted Angela, so she knew where to head in that moment of panicked retreat. She couldn't leave the wedding. If introducing a handsome man wasn't a look she wanted, running away from the wedding would probably be even worse. It was hard to believe she was being forced to convince herself to remain at her friends' wedding. This was a normal adult rite of passage. She ought to be used to it.

But not having friends meant she hadn't been to too many of these, so she hadn't practiced. Since Angela had married nearly as young as Tina had and they weren't at the same college, Tina hadn't even gone to her wedding. Determined to get through the uncomfortable day without causing any further scenes, Tina shoved the handsome guy from her head with a shake and marched toward her friends.

Chapter Two

C lark watched the pretty woman walk away with a slight frown. What an odd encounter. He would have thought she would be as happy as he was to find a friendly person to partner up with for the day. If she had a boyfriend or husband surely, he would have been at her side. And she hadn't claimed to have one, either, just that odd comment about not wanting to sport a certain look, whatever that meant.

With a mental shrug, Clark dismissed the negative thoughts. Maybe she was just one of those man-hating divorcees or she was jealous of the bride or something. Whatever the case, Clark didn't need the negative vibes that day. He fought enough of his own demons, there was certainly no way he was going to take on those of someone he had only encountered by chance at a wedding. While the Cape was little more than a small town, surely it was big enough that he wouldn't have to encounter the snippy woman again, or at least not often.

She had claimed to be friends with both Rachel and Jake, but since he hadn't met her before, they must not be that close. Not to say that he himself was all that close with the couple yet either, but he expected that to change.

He drew himself up short. That was a rather rude, or at least presumptuous, thought. He ought to think that he *hoped* that would change.

Change was hard. But he was determined to do it. It wasn't as though he were eighty-five and thoroughly stuck in his ways like his Grandad. Surely, he could make all the changes he thought necessary. And one of them was to never be rude, not even in his thoughts.

Not to say he had made a habit of rudeness in the past. But his baby brother had often pointed out that his dry wit wasn't the most well received at times. But he had always been the sensitive one. Clark tried not to take his criticism too much to heart.

But nothing had been working for him in the past. It wouldn't hurt him to turn over every leaf there was to find in his attempts at creating a life he could be proud of.

Starting with making friends at this wedding. He stepped forward to greet the next arrivals.

"Hello there," he said with a grin that may have felt forced. "Are you on the groom's side or the bride's?"

Clark might be jealous as all get out of the happy couple that day, but he was determined to smile and enjoy the day. He might want what they had for himself, but he certainly didn't want to take it away from them or in any way detract from their day. In fact, he only wanted to share in their joy. If he could make some friends or even meet a woman while he was at it, it would be an extra win for him.

Not that pretty but grouchy woman he hadn't gotten the name of, but the couple who was just arriving seemed pleasant enough.

Clark was determined. It had been one of his most dominant traits since he was a boy. It had been what got him through his father's leaving the family when he was ten. It had gotten him onto the football team in high school, which had gotten him into a great college. His determination had resulted in a very lucrative career that he had hated. But then it had also made him leave that career behind to start a new life here on Cape Avalon. Clark was going to ensure that his determination got him to a happy life of his own, not leaving him on the sidelines wishing for something else. He had never believed in wishes. Even if you had to fight for it, you had to go out and get what you wanted. He might have missed the boat on marriage and kids in his twenties, but he was far from being an old man, surely it wasn't too late to find a great life for himself if he put his mind to it.

He held out his hand with what he hoped was a warm smile, ready to make some friends. Surely there would be enough people at the wedding he could make at least a couple friends.

Chapter Three

Tina was never so glad of Angela and her husband's welcoming spirit. They had always been kind to her, even when she was her grumpiest self. But they went above and beyond on her behalf at Rachel and Jake's wedding. You would almost think they understood her feelings about marriage. But considering their sickeningly sweet happiness, Tina didn't see how they possibly *could* understand.

Thankfully, Rachel wasn't the most romantic soul on the planet, so the wedding was reasonably straightforward. While it made Tina anxious to listen to them vow before all their friends that they would love each other until death parted them, they didn't linger over any one portion of the ceremony. Jake, of course, lingered over the kiss, but even Tina had to agree that was acceptable at the man's wedding.

Rachel's neighbor had gone crazy with baking for the sweets table, and they had hired a caterer for a savory table. After snacks and well-wishes, the wedding was over. It didn't even take the entire afternoon. Tina was so relieved by the ease of the day that she was able to be pleasant and almost cheerful as she took her leave of the happy couple and even injected sincerity into her voice as she did so.

"You made an exceptionally beautiful bride, Rach," Tina said as she hugged her friend very briefly.

Rachel grinned at the compliment, not bothering to demure. Every bride had a right to be the most gorgeous person in the vicinity on her wedding day. There was something to be said for the glow of happiness.

"I hope you'll be ecstatically happy in your new, joined lives," Tina continued, sounding slightly stilted but meaning every word.

"Did you Google that, Tina?" Jake asked with a grin, teasing her but not bothering to await a reaction. "We certainly will be," he added. "Thanks for coming," he tacked on at the end, even though it was obvious to anyone looking at them that the bride and groom couldn't have cared less if no one had shown up.

Tina's stomach twisted with a disgusting mixture of jealousy and anxiety for her friends. It was a nasty combination. She reminded herself for the umpteenth time that day that she truly was happy for her friends. They were old enough to know their minds, surely. And Rachel had even been married before. If they honestly thought they loved one another, and it was obvious to anyone looking at them that they were head-over-heels, then maybe they really could stick out a life together.

She knew of other success stories. She ought to be confident her friends could be one of them. Just because her own marriage had been a flaming failure didn't mean everyone else's was going to be. Angela's marriage had even started out when they were barely legal, just like her own had. Really, it was rude and quite prideful of her to expect everyone's marriage to fail just because hers had.

But that was her. If you looked up the definition of a certain unpleasant word often attributed to her, you would find quite an accurate description of her. And it

13

included such words as rude and proud. So at least she was consistent and sticking to her personal brand, Tina thought with wry amusement as she finally extricated herself from the small crowd reluctant to leave the new, happy couple.

Tina was genuinely proud of herself in that moment, not the hubris type of proud, but rather, satisfied with her achievement. She had managed to not be the first to leave. She hadn't made any truly sarcastic comments to anyone about anything. And she hadn't disparaged marriage or the wedding in any way. Not out loud, anyway.

For that, she deserved ice cream.

But she was trying to reduce her ice cream intake, she reminded herself with a sigh as she negotiated her small car out of the crowded dead-end street. It was a balancing act. She wanted to lose the excess weight and get all her health markers back into the normal range, but she also needed to reward her good behavior.

Perhaps she would collect her son from her parents' house and take him for a walk and THEN get ice cream. Then it was both a reward and a pleasant outing with Tyler. What with the walk, surely she would deserve those calories. Especially after her good behavior.

But she was trying very hard not to think of food as a reward any longer, so she'd have to reframe that thought. Tina tried not to cuss as she made her way to her parents' place. Transforming your life wasn't any fun and if anyone tried to convince you it was, they were liars. But she was determined to live to a ripe old age, so changes were going to be made, she resolved with a sigh.

Stopped in traffic, Tina tried to smooth out the creases she knew were wrinkling her forehead. She might be thirty-four years old, but she didn't necessarily want to look it. And she certainly didn't want to look any older than that. If it was due to having birthed a child, that was a whole other matter. She would take wrinkles, scars, whatever was needed for bringing and keeping Tyler in the world. Worrying about whether or not she ought to have ice cream and how to express the desire for said ice cream within the silent confines of her own brain, that was not something for which she would allow wrinkles to form.

Should she stop in at the clinic and check on the German Shepherd she had operated on late the evening before?

The errant thought crossed her mind as another wrinkle-forming concern. Tina sighed and reminded herself that she had hired someone for that very reason. Doug might not be the most competent person she'd ever met, but he knew how to dial a phone. If the dog was in any sort of distress, Tina was confident she would have heard from him.

For a while now, she had been trying to make changes in her life. She hadn't yet found full success, but Doug was one of those efforts. She was trying to make more time for Tyler. He was already turning into a little man. She wasn't going to have so great an influence over him for much longer. And so, Tina was determined to make as many amazing memories with him as she could, for both his benefit and her own. But if there were any animals needing to remain at the clinic overnight, someone had to be there. In the past, she had taken that on herself. Here on the island, there weren't so many pets that she was overrun with business. Tina refused to accept it was her acerbic personality keeping away paying pet parents. But perhaps if she had a little more rest, she'd be less cranky. And then she might draw more patients to her practice.

Or, maybe, she'd be able to figure out a good way of drawing more business without needing to leave the island. It was one of the best things about living and working on the island. When things were quiet, she could leave. And she wasn't far from home no matter where she was. She also wasn't far from the beach no matter where she was on the island. It was why she had come home after college and that one exciting year in New York.

There might have been the greatest variety of animals to treat when she lived in New York, but nothing could beat raising her son on Cape Avalon. The small-town vibe meant most of Tyler's friends were the children of people she at least had a passing acquaintance with, either through her clinic or from her own childhood.

Too, being nearer to her parents was proving to be mutually beneficial. They had helped her out with Tyler, and now she was starting to help them out with things that needed doing. Mostly, so far, her involvement had been confined to hiring help for them whenever it was needed, but the sad fact was that her parents were aging. There was going to come a time that they'd need more help than they were giving.

She was certainly not complaining about that. It was the great equalizing she expected. They had given way more than their share in her lifetime. Tina was uncomfortably aware that most adults in their thirties hadn't needed to rely on their parents as much as she had thus far. If her parents needed her in the future, whatever they needed, she would give them. They had certainly earned her undying gratitude.

But she hated to feel indebted.

She wished she could pay in a tangible way. But her parents didn't need her money, even if she managed to amass any amount of it. Not that she had. She was just finally getting out from beneath the burden of student loans. Longer than others her age, she was sure. But most people her age didn't have an eleven-year-old son they'd raised alone. It was fortunate that she had been nearly finished with school when her husband had died. She was completely finished with the school portion of her education by the time Tyler was born. That she had been able to find a paid internship was extra fortunate. It hadn't paid much, but she had been able to find a tiny little flat for her and Tyler and a very cheap daycare willing to take an infant.

Tina shuddered to think of what sort of conditions Tyler had spent time in during that adventurous six months until she had been fully accredited and had been able to make a little more money in order to find them a better place to live and nicer daycare. But they had survived and even thrived there in New York. But once Tyler was a bit bigger, it had started to bother Tina that he was so confined. On Cape Avalon he could have a yard and his grandparents and the beach. No, it wasn't a wonderful, massive, multicultural city, but Tina figured it was better for him despite those lacks. If she had been able to afford a yard or even to live near a nicer park or playground, she might've stayed in the city. But when her parents suggested she might be able to start a veterinary clinic on the island and they'd help her with Tyler, she had decided to give it a shot.

Almost nine years later, they were still here.

Tina doubted Tyler even remembered their time in New York. That was one of the things she was hoping to change. Not that she could make his little mind recall their time in the city. And maybe his memories wouldn't be as great as hers were anyway. But she was planning to make more memories with him. If she had help in the clinic, she could take Tyler for little trips now and again. Really, New York was only a few hours away; they could make a weekend out of it whenever they wanted. Even with the population growth on the Cape, she doubted she would ever be so busy that she couldn't get away, as long as she had someone she could rely on to watch over any overnight creatures when that happened.

Tina actually found herself smiling as she neared her parents' house. She had things to look froward to. Her friends' wedding had seemed to please them. Life was good. She would convince herself of it soon, she was sure.

Chapter Four

B ut her boy still needed a man to do manly things with.

Tina sighed late that night, as she picked up the form she had turned face down on her dresser that morning. It had been all Tyler wanted to talk about on their walk at the beach. Big Brother this and Big Brother that.

The thought of entrusting her son to a stranger made Tina want to eat a pint of Ben and Jerry's or a full-size bag of potato chips. But she steeled her nerves and read the form again.

She tried her best, but for one thing, she was still too busy despite her efforts to cut back. She still needed to do all the things other homeowners had to do. While Tyler was getting big enough to help her with some of those things, she didn't want him to become the man of the house just yet. So, she had to be both housekeeper and handyman. Tyler helped often and they could make a game of it. But it still occupied a lot of time that he could be off adventuring if they were a two-parent household.

And she really didn't have a great deal of interest in football, hockey, soccer, or camping – all the things Tyler longed to explore. Tina couldn't afford to put him in all of those activities all the time. That was one of Tyler's arguments in support of getting a Big Brother.

He wouldn't have to join anything, but he could get a chance to play some of those sports or at least get a little practice or exposure. Then he could maybe sign up for one rather than all of them.

Tina was fairly certain her son was going to be a negotiator when he grew up. She wasn't sure which fields hired negotiators, but it was evident Tyler would be successful at it.

One more thing she needed to look into. But she had time. He wouldn't be heading to college for another eight years. And even then, he didn't have to know for certain what he wanted to be when he got done.

She just had to keep his life complication free. No young marriages for him, that was for certain. But she had no regrets, she reminded herself, even if she was a dark and twisted shadow of her former self. Tyler was worth everything.

And really, dark wasn't the worst thing. They said dark chocolate was better for you than white or milk chocolate, so there was that little tidbit.

Not that she would be indulging in any, she reminded herself as temptation rolled through her. Just because she was experiencing feelings didn't mean she needed to smother them in food, especially not anything that was likely to spike her blood sugar or her cholesterol.

Deep breath in, hold for four, breathe out for four, in for four... Low and behold, those stupid breathing exercises often worked, much to her shock. Another walk would probably do her good and help distract her from both her worries and her snack attack. But she wasn't comfortable leaving Tyler in the house by himself, at least not while he was asleep and thus extra vulnerable. While it was true that many of the things she feared might happen to him had never actually ever occurred on the Cape, she didn't want to take a chance on their being the first victims.

Perhaps she could find a video online she could do. Like an exercise video. She hadn't done one of those since her cross-country days in high school. But this was a high school throwback kind of day, so why not? She searched and found something that appeared as though it wouldn't be too difficult and started her twenty-minute sweat session. According to what she had researched, if she could put off a craving for twenty minutes it would pass. If it didn't, maybe she really was hungry. And she had finally gone to the step of stocking the house with healthier snacks rather than her favorite chips and cookies. Tyler didn't even seem to mind the change. She had been blessed by being given the most easy-going kid on the planet. She certainly wouldn't have been so accepting of the house being cleared of junk food when she had been his age.

As she wheezed her way through the video in all her uncoordinated glory, she started to think that maybe she *could* learn to camp and play hockey. But when she finally got to the end of the video and allowed herself to sink to the floor in a giant sweaty lump, she realized she had absolutely no desire to do so. Yes, she wanted to get herself into better shape so she could live to see her son grow up. No, she did not want to learn how to camp. She was certain it wasn't that difficult, but she still had no desire to engage in such an activity. She would consider hiking, but that was as close to wilderness engagement she wanted to get. Bugs were one of her least favorite things.

She had tried so hard and still managed to barely tolerate it when Tyler, as a little boy, was fascinated with insects and creeping critters. She had staved off his intense desire to have the things as pets, but she had to compensate for that loss by taking him for field trips to such disgusting places as Insect World and Reptile Place. She had considered taking nerve-numbing medications on those occasions but had managed to numb the anxiety with chips and soda to get through the experiences.

It was a relief that Tyler had moved on from those interests in some ways. But now that she was trying to learn other coping skills, a part of her longed for the days of trips to bug land. Despite her phobias, she would take tarantulas over strange men in her son's life.

That was probably why she had never dated.

Or maybe it was because she was an unhealthy, cranky wreck.

It didn't matter, her son loved her despite everything. He was her one true, great accomplishment.

After a few more stretches, Tina managed to pull herself off the floor and into the shower. She burned in muscles she had never realized she possessed. That was probably a good thing in a certain way, but she might regret her choices in the morning.

No, she couldn't regret making healthier choices even if there were a few aches and pains along with it. She was going to live to see her son grow up even if it killed her in the process. She managed to smile over the obtuse thought.

It was time. More than time. There were changes Tina was determined to make. Having just made her last payment on all her debts aside from her mortgage, Tina felt it was the perfect time to make those fresh starts. Getting her health in line was just the beginning.

Finally, after her shower and a cup of camomile tea, she was able to read the permission form without having a nervous breakdown and craving all the snacks. Taking careful note of the fact that all candidates submitted a background check, police verification, and the parent could accompany the duo on their first couple of outings if they so wished, Tina finally signed away her permission.

Tyler had been asking and begging for a month. The fact that he had persisted indicated how very much he wanted the experience. It pained Tina that she couldn't be enough for her son, but she had to accept it and move on. She ought to be grateful there were such programs available to fill such needs. She actually wouldn't have expected it in such a community as Cape Avalon. Not that it was so very small, but it was far from a metropolis. Tina had no idea what the population actually was, but she wouldn't have thought it was large enough to warrant such a provision.

A part of her, not the part that was a mother to a child wanting to join the program, but the objective part of her, thought the program was amazing. She loved their motto of helping change kids' perspectives and giving them opportunities to reach their potential. It was perfect. For someone else's kid. Tina sighed.

It didn't matter how reluctant she might be. The Cape *was* big enough to warrant such a program. And Tyler knew about it. So, she had been stuck with staring at the form and making the heavy decision. Her parents were great. They had helped her and Tyler immensely, especially when they had first moved back to Cape Avalon and Tyler was still too young for school. They had taken over all his childcare needs for her while she was at work. That was the only way she had been able to afford a house and her student loans on a single income.

Now, her loans were finally paid off and she was able to cut back on her working hours a bit. But she was still just one woman. And Tyler was craving a male influence that even her father's love couldn't provide. If only her dad were ten years younger, he might be able to do all the things Tyler was wishing for. But wishes weren't going to get them anywhere.

With a knot in her stomach, Tina reviewed the form once more before putting it out on the table so Tyler could see it in the morning. She would definitely be reviewing the criminal background check and going on their first excursions with whoever the service paired Tyler with.

The next morning, after a restless sleep, Tina was awakened by a joyful whoop coming from the kitchen. Tyler was up and had seen the form, evidently.

"Mom, Mom, Mom!" he called, running into her room, and jumping on her bed like he had when he was smaller. He hadn't done such things in over a year, so it brought a lump to Tina's throat that she quickly swallowed and ignored.

"I heard you the first time," she grumbled even as she pulled him in to snuggle.

"Thank you," he said simply, moderating his volume. "I didn't think you were going to."

Tina had to cough to get past the clog of the threat of tears. She had never been a weeper. She wasn't going to start now.

"Sorry I took so long. I hope it isn't going to hold you back from getting matched. But it was a tough decision for me, kiddo."

"I know, Mom. But I'm glad you finally made it. I know it's going to be awesome."

"You know, huh? How do you know?"

"One of the kids in my class signed up and they've already been playing football and even went camping one weekend."

Tina's stomach clenched anew. If she had to accompany Tyler and some strange man on a camping trip, this was going to be a serious chore. But she would do it. There was no way she was letting Tyler go off alone with a stranger for a weekend in the woods. It was one of the things Tyler most wanted to do and she was least qualified for. So, she ought to be more grateful for the program.

She would get there eventually. For now, she would be satisfied with not throwing up on her son's curly head.

"What did you want to do today, kiddo?" she finally asked, changing the tone of her thoughts.

"Want to go to the beach? Or ride our bikes?" Tyler asked eagerly. "Or do we have to do chores all day?" he asked, his voice changing to one of determination but filled with disappointment.

"How about I make pancakes first, then let's do a few little chores, just to make sure everything is ready for the week, then right after lunch we'll go ride our bikes to the beach?"

"That sounds perfect, Mom, you're the best."

Tina's heart expanded almost painfully as his little arms wrapped around her and she again swallowed the threat of tears. His arms weren't so very little anymore, she noticed as she held him close. He was going to be taller than she was in a few years. They wouldn't be sharing such snuggles much longer. As it was, even now, it was a rarity. She would take her blessings where she could get them. She had been so fortunate with her boy. He was as helpful as he could be and not overly demanding. She should have signed his stupid form before now.

"I'm sorry I took so long," she muttered again. "I just was so worried about it."

"I know, Mom, don't worry about that part. I'm sure they'll still have someone for me. And I know you are just looking out for me."

"How did you get so wise?"

Tyler had already sat up and was swinging his feet over the side of the bed. His shrug wasn't as nonchalant as he probably intended. Tina could tell he was bashful from her praise. But she meant every word of it.

The day flew by. After sleeping in and devouring a stack of pancakes made from almond flour that weren't nearly as gross as she thought they were going to be, they hurried through the various chores that needed to be done regularly. Tyler mowed their small yard while she cleaned their two bathrooms. Tyler did a quick mop of the floors and dusting at least what was visible while she folded a couple loads of laundry and whipped them up a health-conscious lunch of cold chicken and vegetable sticks.

And then they were off on their bicycles.

Tina had spent her adult life feeling grumpy about anything that generated sweat. But her son needed activity, and she was willing to admit that she did, too. If she was serious about getting her weight and cholesterol and everything else the doctor had mentioned under control, she needed lots of activity. There was only so much good genes and spandex could do for her. It wasn't going to lower her cholesterol or help her liver or whatever other organ was involved in controlling your blood sugar. Only proper eating and exercise were going to do that.

Now was the time, or so the doctor had said. If she could start things moving in the right direction before she hit thirty-five, she had a much better chance of living to meet her grandchildren. Otherwise, according to the doctor's dire warnings, there was a good chance heart disease was in her future.

That was *not* something she wanted to experiment with. She had seen the effects of obesity on her animals. She certainly didn't want to put herself through the sorts of treatments she put her patients through. She knew what she had to do.

And so it was that she tried very hard not to grimace whenever Tyler looked over his shoulder at her and smiled encouragingly. He was such a dear boy, hanging back so as to not get too far ahead of her. But she was doing her best. She tried not to beat herself up over her inadequacies. At least she was out there trying. She could have stayed at home and read a book or watched movies. No, she was out there sweating like some disgusting gym rat, but the grin on her son's face was nearly worth it.

Keep your eyes on the end goal.

One of Rachel's stupid peppy motivational quotes popped into Tina's head as she thought about getting off to walk her bike up the small incline. Gritting her teeth, she stood up on the pedals and kept going on the bicycle. Never mind that it wasn't even really a hill. She was out of shape and tired. If she could make it to the top without getting off, she would be inordinately proud of herself.

But Rachel's stupid quote fit for many areas of her life – reducing her hours of work, getting healthy, allowing Tyler to go off with a stranger, trying to stop being the Wicked Witch of the West, or perhaps she ought to think of herself as the Wicked Witch of the East, since Cape Avalon jutted out into the Atlantic.

That thought finally helped her see something funny about her day, and her small smile spread into a wide grin as she finally reached the top to find Tyler patiently waiting for her. Of course, she could barely see him for the spots that were dancing in front of her eyes from the exertion and lack of oxygen. But she had done it. It was a very small step in the right direction.

"Way to go, Mom! You didn't even stop," Tyler crowed from his spot on the side of the road as Tina slowed and got off her bike on rubbery legs.

"Does it undo my effort if I get off now?"

"Nope," Tyler insisted. "Can't take away accomplishments. They're already done, that's why they're called accomplishments."

Tina shook her head over the ten-year-old's wisdom. He wasn't wrong. And she was ridiculously proud of her little accomplishment.

"Are we almost there?" she asked as they climbed back onto their bicycles after stretching out their muscles. Tyler's laugh didn't fill Tina with confidence, but she didn't ask for any clarification.

She survived the rest of the journey to the shore and was able to rest on a blanket while Tyler played in the waves. It wasn't hot enough for Tina to join him. That water was too often frigidly cold. She used to force herself to go in when Tyler was smaller and needed the accompaniment. But now he could happily entertain himself in the surf with her only needing to keep half an eye on him, just in case.

The worried mom in her wanted to never take her eyes off him for a second, but the part of her that was trying to be a reasonable person and have a little sliver of a life for herself realized she had to let him have fun and she could enjoy her book at least for a few minutes.

The beach wasn't very busy that day, which was a surprise for such a beautiful weekend day. Of course, they had chosen one of the less popular beaches, one that it seemed only locals knew about, but still, there weren't even many locals out today. Anxiety nibbled at her. Had she forgotten about something amazing going on somewhere that she ought to be taking Tyler to see?

Tina took a deep breath and held it for a moment while running the fingers of her free hand, that wasn't holding the book, through the sand, trying to ground herself into the moment.

Even if there was something going on, she and Tyler were having a great day. She was glad they weren't doing anything else. And if there was something awesome or exciting enough, Tyler would have made sure she knew about it. She was not scarring her son for life by taking him to the beach rather than to wherever her neighbors were going that day.

Shaking her head, Tina turned her attention back to her book. But it wasn't all that interesting. Or maybe the view was just better. But she would honestly rather watch Tyler playing. If it were a few degrees warmer, she would even join him. But she didn't want to freeze her muscles right off, even if that might be good treatment to help them recover from the strain of the ride there.

While she was staring off into the surf, Tyler ran toward her and flopped down on the blanket in the boneless way children had.

"Did you have fun?"

"I did," he said with a grin, "but my toes were getting cold."

"Only your toes?" Tina asked with a chuckle.

Tyler laughed but shrugged. "Did we bring any snacks?"

"We have water, grapes, and almonds."

"Yummm," Tyler replied promptly and waited while his mother rustled in her backpack.

They sat in companionable silence while they munched for a minute, both staring out at the sandpipers dodging the constant flow of the water.

"Do you miss chips sometimes?" Tyler asked, making Tina laugh.

"Every single day," Tina replied immediately.

Tyler nodded. "I don't miss it every day, but every once in a while I get a sudden craving."

"Sorry, kiddo. I don't know if I have the willpower to keep a supply for you."

"That's ok, Mom. I don't really need them. I think fruit and stuff is good, too. It's nice for a change. But you didn't really talk about it before you got rid of everything. Are you sick or something?"

"Not yet," Tina answered slowly, hesitant to be fully honest with her son. But taking a deep breath, she told him the truth. "But the doctor told me if I didn't make some changes, I would have serious problems soon. I probably should have warned you before we went cold turkey, but I was afraid any resistance from you might make me chicken out. Thanks for being so cool about it."

Tyler shrugged again. "I can always get a fix at Gramma and Grampa's house," he told her with a grin. "And I would hate to see you get really sick."

Tina nodded. "Yeah, I need to get myself in shape now, while I can. Apparently eating too many chips and not getting enough exercise can clog up your arteries, and then your blood doesn't want to flow freely like it should. So, I'm trying to prevent that from happening."

Tyler looked at her with his nose wrinkled adorably. "What would happen if your blood didn't flow right? That doesn't sound good."

"Yeah, it's not great. But you have nothing to worry about. I'm not going to let that happen. That's why I got rid of all the chips. That's my biggest weakness and also the worst thing in these situations." Tina could see that Tyler was worrying despite her words, so she tried to be a little more honest with him. "I need to lose a bit of weight and learn to eat more fruit and vegetables instead of chips and cake. You really don't need to worry about this. I know you won't believe this, but I'm not actually all that old so from what the doctor said, if I can get on top of these problems now, there shouldn't be any long-term effects."

"So, you won't die like my dad did?" Tyler asked quietly, not quite meeting her eye.

"I'd like to say I'll never die, but certainly not until you're old and fully sick of me."

Tyler threw himself at her like the little boy he used to be. "I'll never be sick of you, Mommy."

Tina squeezed him tight and tried hard to swallow around the lump that threatened to choke her throat. "You're the best boy, Tyler." She squeezed him again and then let him wriggle back out of her arms. "But seriously, you really don't have to worry about this. You are affected because I'm changing the way we eat a little bit, and I'll need your help to get a bit more active, like we did today. But other than that, nothing is changing."

"Well, except that I'm going to get my Big Brother."

Tina felt her smile thin at the mention of the scary program. She tried to be enthusiastic about it, but she couldn't help asking some questions of her own. "You aren't nervous about spending time with a stranger?"

Tyler frowned. "Well, he won't be a total stranger, right? The school will know him. It's like when I get a new teacher at the start of the school year, isn't it? Everyone is a little nervous until we get to know the teacher, but he was hired by the school so it's not like he's some random guy in a van with a puppy trying to lure little kids from the playground."

Her laugh sounded a little forced, but Tina didn't care. It was a good analogy. And Tyler had hit her concerns exactly on the head. "You make a good point. I've never worried about your teachers. But you're also never alone with any of your teachers."

"I might be alone with the guidance counselor sometime. Or the principal."

Tina nodded, again seeing her son's point. "All right, all right. I already signed the permission slip."

"And it's safely tucked inside my backpack so it can't get lost before tomorrow morning."

Tina laughed again. This time it sounded rusty because it was truly genuine. She rarely felt an urge for genuine amusement. But her kid brought out the best in her, unlike everyone else she encountered.

"I hope it won't embarrass you that I intend to avail myself of the provision to accompany the two of you on your first couple of times together."

Tyler lifted one shoulder. "Is that what made you agree?"

"Pretty much," Tina admitted. "That and the fact that you wouldn't let it go. That told me how much it meant to you."

Tyler nodded. "If that's the only way you could say yes, then I'll try not to be too embarrassed about it. But you better not tell him any stories about me as a baby."

Tina laughed again. "Maybe I'll find some really great pictures of you." She looked at him with widened eyes. "What a great idea, thanks Tyler!"

"Mom!" He tried to sound as though he were whining, but he must have realized she was joking as he quickly dissolved into laughter.

Without conscious thought, they both ended up on their backs staring up at the sky and they resumed an old game they had always played, seeing imaginary things in the clouds.

"Mushrooms," Tyler called out, pointing.

"Bugs Bunny," Tina countered, pointing in the opposite direction.

"Really? Where?" Tyler demanded, trying to follow the line of her finger.

The rest of the afternoon faded, and soon it was time to head home. Tina had put the bike ride off long enough. They would be too hungry to eat healthy if they didn't get going now. But her backside was not looking forward to climbing back onto the extremely hard seat of her bicycle.

Chapter Five

S he survived the ride, just barely. But despite the pain in all parts of her body, Tina was ridiculously proud of herself. She hadn't been physically active since she was a student. Of course, she had tried to keep up with Tyler throughout his life, but she had often just strolled behind him yelling encouragement rather than actually staying right with him. Unlike that day when she had, for the most part, stayed right alongside him, except for that hill that nearly killed her.

They had agreed to do it again as many times as they could that week, after school or after supper. Tyler was eager to help and also thrilled at the thought of getting to go biking so much. Tina was relieved that he wasn't whining about missing his shows. What a disappointment to find out that the television addiction was hers alone. If she hadn't received this wake-up call brought on by her search for a new insurance provider, she would have been the source of her darling son's physical problems eventually.

She tried not to beat herself up about it, but that seemed to be her default setting. She tried to think of an affirmation to combat the negative thoughts.

You can only do what you can do. Tina had to laugh. It was a little half-hearted, which the affirmations her friend Rachel used were far from. Rachel favored over the top, powerful, warrior-type affirmations like *You are Queen of the World.* She probably wouldn't approve of *You can only do what you can do.* But Tina actually quite liked it. Especially for such a circumstance as this. She had always tried to do her best, especially when it came to Tyler, but she was only one very weak human. She could only do what she could do. If she could manage to do better now, that was fabulous, but she would have to try to forgive herself for the past. Or at least ignore it as thoroughly as possible. It wouldn't benefit any of them for her to ruminate on it.

Again, she almost laughed as she thought of the word she'd just used. Ruminate. Would that be a veterinarian word or was that her author friend's wordy influence? Either way, it was the perfect word for the situation. Cows ruminate when they chew their cud. Humans ruminate when they worry a subject to death. She didn't want to be a cow. And worrying about the past wasn't benefiting her in the least. It had to stop.

She certainly wasn't going to give any thoughts to her dead husband that evening.

Thinking about him and his treatment of her would send her to the secret stash of Ben and Jerry's she had saved, hidden behind the frozen vegetables for emergency situations. This was not an emergency. She was merely feeling muscles that hadn't exerted themselves in years. Perhaps a warm bath with Epsom salts would be in order.

After making a healthy yet kid-approved meal, Tina was satisfied to see that the house and its residents were ready for the coming week. She said goodnight to Tyler early, telling him she was going for a soak and wasn't sure how long it would take.

35

Tyler cast her a worried frown. "Are you very sore?"

"I am, but that is probably to be expected. Even walking made me super sore the first couple of times. Now I can do that pretty good. So don't worry about it."

"Are you sure? Do you want me to get you some ibuprofen?"

Tina laughed and shook her head. "No, no. I'm trying to shrink my gut, not burn it off with acid. The bath should do the trick just fine."

Tyler didn't look convinced, but he didn't press the matter.

"Don't stay up too late," she called after kissing him goodnight and leaving the room. His laughter followed her into her own room with its en-suite bathroom. She was usually the irresponsible one who stayed up all hours. She had been having sleep issues for years. But since she started exercising a little bit and eating better, she had also been sleeping better. So, Tyler's laughter was justified.

He was such a good, responsible kid. It was one more thing Tina worried about. He was probably too responsible. She should have been more parental toward him. She should have set a stronger role model lead. Not allowing him to take on so many chores and such.

You can only do what you can do.

Tina's worried frown slipped into something that approximated a smile.

With a bit of a shrug Tina supposed there was nothing really wrong with a ten-year-old boy knowing how to be responsible. But she would do her very best to ensure he also got to have more fun. Manly fun. The type she had little interest in having with him. He, of course, did on occasion spend time with boys from his class that he was friends with, but he had never been included in his friends' father-son excursions. Perhaps she should have made a bigger push to arrange for that sort of thing.

Tina shrugged mentally. The decision had already been made. Tyler would sign up for a Big Brother. But she would do everything in her considerable willpower to ensure he was safe. She would accompany him and whichever grown boy the school paired him with and bear up under whichever grossly male activity they chose to participate in, and she would check out this other male and only once she was certain she could trust him, would she allow her son to spend time with him without her.

Thus resolved, and with her bathwater finally growing tepid, Tina felt able to go to bed. To her surprise, she slept the sleep of the dead. It was the first time in at least twelve years that she had slept so soundly. It would seem a healthy life was going to agree with her after all, at least some parts.

The day dawned bright and clear, another gorgeous day on Cape Avalon. Tina chatted with Angela on the Bluetooth in her car on the way to the clinic after dropping Tyler at her parents' house.

"Wasn't the wedding romantic?" Angela had almost cooed. Tina's stomach clenched in disgust.

"Rachel was a beautiful bride," she managed to reply with sincerity.

"I can't believe how in love she and Jake are. Who'd have thought after how they behaved in high school?"

That led Tina to a light chuckle. "You're the one who studied psychology. You probably should have been able to guess with your degree. Don't boys always act out when they have a crush on a girl?"

Angela laughed good naturedly along with Tina. "True. You've got a point there. Do you think they'll have kids?"

"It wouldn't surprise me terribly," Tina answered. "Rachel isn't too old. And Jake seems devoted to his niece, so it's likely he wants kids."

"Nieces and kids of your own are two different things."

"I guess we'll have to wait and see. I've actually enjoyed having Rachel back on the Cape and in our small circle."

Angela laughed again. "I know! It's still a surprise to me when I think of it. You never wanted to let anyone else into our circle before."

Tina shrugged even if Angela couldn't see her. "It could be argued she was already in the circle since she was in our class in school."

Angela just laughed again and changed the subject. "What do you have going on today?"

"I'm neutering a cat and spaying a dog this morning. And someone is bringing in a bunny that's losing his fur inexplicably."

"Aww, poor thing. What do you think is wrong with it?"

Tina shrugged again before shaking her head at herself for being silly. "I'm afraid it might be stress. This family has several small children. If they haven't been taught to be gentle with the little thing, it could be as simple as that. But I won't know until I see it."

"So, do you think you'll have time for lunch or a coffee today?"

"My lunch is going to consist of vegetable sticks today, but I'd love to grab a coffee at some point. I don't remember what time my appointments were scheduled for and there might be other things that crept in without my knowledge. I'll give you a call after I've reviewed my calendar when I get to the office."

"Sounds good. You know my schedule is flexible. I just need to be home by two o'clock for the youngest urchin's return."

Tina laughed again. "Must be nice to be a kept woman."

"It's lovely," Angela replied immediately. "But from what I know of you, you wouldn't like it. With all your nervous, angry energy, you'd vibrate your walls down."

Rather than being offended, her friend's words amused her immensely. "You're probably right. Although, perhaps I wouldn't be so angry if I was kept by a man as great as yours."

"Paws off, sister," Angela answered with a good-natured growl, knowing full well Tina had no designs on her husband.

"Seriously, though, Ang, you know I'm happy for both you and Rachel, despite my feelings to the contrary on the matter."

"Of course, I know. I am fully aware that under your hard shell you're actually a softie."

"Don't tell the others," Tina concluded with a laugh as she pulled into the parking lot of her clinic. "I'll call you back soon, I'm here and it looks like there are already patients waiting for me."

"Uh oh, animal emergencies are never good. Talk soon," Angela said right away and hung up without awaiting a reply.

Tina smiled a little despite the worry that threatened at the sight of the waiting cars. She might not have many friends, but the ones she had were the best.

It took two hours for her to deal with the minor emergencies that had been waiting for her on her arrival. Thankfully they truly were minor but squeezing them in around the appointments that had been already booked made the morning more hectic than she had expected, and she almost forgot about Angela's invitation for coffee.

"Am I too late to take you up on the offer for a coffee break?"

Angela's good humor came through the phone clearly. "I was hoping you'd ask. I'm just pulling into the parking lot. Want to just grab something here?"

Tina had to smile. Angela was the best friend a grumpy introvert could ask for. She hung up the phone and hurried out of the clinic, not bothering to change out of her scrubs. It would give her more time to relax with her friend.

"What does one order when they are trying to reduce their fat or cholesterol?" Tina asked as she stared at the menu in the small café in the same strip as her clinic.

"You could try just getting a plain old coffee like the old-fashioned people order," Angela suggested with a chuckle. "Or even tea? Are we old enough for tea yet?"

"I need the kick of caffeine, I think. After the crazy morning I'm having, tea might not cut it for me."

"Ask the barista, he'd know, for sure. There are probably all sorts of non-sugar, no-fat options that might still have some flavor to them."

Tina rolled her eyes but did as her friend suggested and soon found herself sipping a very complicated sounding but deliciously caffeinated hot beverage that the young man at the counter assured her would not add too much to her calorie count nor her cholesterol levels. She should have paid closer attention to what he had said, she would like to drink it again.

"There's a sticker on the side," Angela pointed out drily. "You could always keep that for next time."

"You are brilliant, thank you."

Angela laughed and turned the topic. "How was the rest of your weekend? You didn't tell me what you and Tyler had planned."

"After the wedding we just chilled out at home, but Sunday was fantastic. We did a bunch of chores in the morning and then rode our bikes out to the beach. I thought I was going to die trying to get up the hills, but we made it there and back, and I am still alive to tell the tale."

"What hills?" Angela asked, puzzled. "Where did you go?"

"Don't get cute and technical, Ang. You work out with your athlete husband, so you can't exactly relate to my situation."

"But I'd like to understand," Angela argued. "I'm not being sarcastic, I just didn't think before I asked, my apologies. Are you still worried about what the doctor told you?"

"Of course, I am. Tyler doesn't have anyone but me. My parents have been amazing to us, but I can't leave him to them full-time. I have to get healthy for Tyler, if nothing else."

"Don't I get a vote?"

Tina grinned. Her friend was such a loyal person, it was one of her best traits.

"So, what's your plan, anyway, besides bike rides and low-fat coffee beverages?"

"Tyler and I are trying to eliminate chips and cookies from the house. Or rather, I'm trying to eliminate them, and Tyler isn't objecting. Chips especially were my main weakness. And we're going to try to ride our bikes every day or as many days each week as we can, weather and schedule permitting. And ice cream will be a treat that can only be eaten away from home. Like we can buy a cone, but not keep pints at home in the freezer."

Angela was nodding encouragingly, so Tina continued. "Other than that, just trying to increase the fruits and vegetables in our diet and decrease the deep frying. I don't know. The doctor said at my age I should be able to make a full recovery, but I feel like I've always been fat and sluggish. I don't see how I can just turn it around."

"You aren't that heavy, even now, Tina. And you were just as thin as everyone else when we were doing track and field in school. I'm sure there's an athlete inside you just waiting to come out."

"There might one hiding under all of this," Tina replied with sarcasm, gesturing toward her belly.

Ever loyal, Angela didn't appreciate Tina's comment. "Don't be like that, Tina. You need to learn to start talking better to and about yourself."

"Now you're starting to sound just like Rachel."

"Well, she was always the smartest one in our group."

Tina appreciated her friend's support even though she didn't know how to express that appreciation. She cleared her throat to skip over the awkward moment.

"How are you and Mr. Hunk and the kids?"

"Everyone's good. We had a good weekend, too. Maybe not as productive as yours, but there was swimming included."

"Nice," Tina remarked. "Did you have another community pool party?"

Angela nodded. "We did. I'll admit, after the wedding on Saturday and that on Sunday, I'm a little peopled out."

"I didn't think you had it in you to get peopled out," Tina marveled. "That's more my thing."

"Well, I understand it a little more now," Angela said with a light laugh. "It's one thing to be happy to always have my friends around and quite another to spend two days with people I haven't specifically chosen." She laughed again as though embarrassed to admit to such feelings. "I mean, everyone was nice and everything, of course. It's not as though Rachel and Jake would have anyone unpleasant at their wedding, but I realize more now that with your longer time friends you have more of a short-hand, not everything needs to be fully explained or spelled out. That's not at all true of brand-new acquaintances. Even neighbors, like in our community, there's so many we don't know well. So, it's a bit more tense. I'm quite exhausted."

"Plus, I'm sure, you were busy being hostess on top of the socializing, right?"

Angela shrugged. She was always the best hostess. "It actually helped me feel more comfortable if I had a plate of something in my hand at all times to offer others. Like an ice breaker."

"I would have just eaten it all myself as a way of making myself more comfortable."

"Which is why you are finding new sources of comfort, right?"

Tina sighed and nodded. "Let's rather say I'm trying. It's hard when the discomfort is so well embedded and deep-fried food as the go-to coping mechanism has been an ingrained behavior since childhood."

"But since you're trying to break all the stereotypes and so on for Tyler's sake, you will keep searching, right?"

Tina looked at Angela closely. "Have you been revisiting your psyche classes or something?"

"No, just reading some books on the subject."

"Why?"

"You aren't the only one with issues, for one thing," Angela started sounding almost defensive. "But really,

I just want to be a good friend. Since you told me about your numbers, I've done some research."

"You've always been the best friend a gal could ask for." Tina said it with all sincerity. Not that she had other friends, but Angela had always been there for her, supportive and caring no matter how grouchy Tina might be.

Angela shook her head. "A true friend doesn't just tell you what you want to hear, she tells you what you *need* to hear."

Tina narrowed her eyes. "You aren't going to start mothering me now, are you?"

Angela laughed. "Not at all. But I do want to know how to help you on this journey. For example, I probably shouldn't have asked you for coffee, but instead to go for a walk."

"We'll get there eventually," Tina said. "Remember, baby steps." But then she reached over and grasped her friend's hand for a moment. "Thanks, though, Ang. I mean it. Your support does mean the world to me."

Angela's happy smile nearly split her face. "I need to make sure you stick around longer than me," she said with another one of her pleasant laughs. "If you were to die before me, where would I be then?"

Tina's laugh sounded more like a bark, but it didn't get used nearly as often as Angela's. She glanced at her watch.

"I need to get back soon, but can I ask you something?"

Angela's gaze sharpened on her face. "Of course, always."

"Would you let your kids join Brownies or whatever?"

Angela's nose wrinkled. "They haven't expressed an interest."

"But would you let them if they did? Or some other type of thing that would see them going off with an adult you don't know?"

Angela searched Tina's face. "Does Tyler want to be a Scout?"

Tina shook her head. "I wish it was that simple. Then there'd at least be a bunch of other kids."

"So, what is it exactly that you're asking about?"

"This Big Brother arrangement that their school is coordinating. Tyler wants it so bad, and the very thought curdles my stomach and makes me want to hit things. But I finally signed the permission slip for him Saturday night, and he's beside himself with happiness today." Tina sighed, took a sip of her cooling coffee drink, and made a face. "So, for how happy he is, I feel I made the right decision, but it's so scary and risky to let him go off with a strange man."

"Of course, that does sound terrifying. But do they do background checks on everyone?"

"They do, of course, but just because he has good credit and hasn't been caught doing anything criminal in the past doesn't mean he isn't going to start now. I mean, in a certain way, what kind of guy would sign up for this type of thing in the first place? I guess that's really what has me worried."

"What do you mean?"

"Like, what kind of man has the time and inclination to sign up to mentor young fatherless boys? It makes me think he'll either be a total loser or worse."

Angela laughed a little over Tina's words, but she gave the matter serious thought. "I can understand your worries, of course. But it's possible the men who sign up for such a program were in a similar situation themselves. Maybe they've grown up without a father or strong male influence but have managed to pull themselves to a place of success and want to give back to their community in some way. And knowing how to navigate the world they experienced, they want to give a leg up to someone else, so the youngster doesn't face the same challenges they themselves did. Or perhaps they suffered a loss, like their child died or a younger sibling. There are any number of sad, but perfectly harmless reasons a man might want to be available for something like this."

"Wow, spoken like a true psyche major. But your words give me hope, thanks Ang. I should have talked to you about it sooner, but I was too caught up in the wedding to ask you about this."

Angela nodded. "I wanted to ask you, was the wedding as bad as you thought it would be?"

"For the most part, no. You and your hottie are happy even after all these years, right?"

Angela grinned and Tina could almost see stars in her eyes, which filled her for a brief moment with very green envy but she pushed the unwelcome sensation away. She might be the grouchiest vet on earth, but she wasn't going to alienate her only friend. She kept her mind on the topic, or rather the aspect of the topic, at hand. If she went down the rabbit hole of her own past, she'd have a breakdown. "So, it's entirely possible that Rachel and Jake will be happy too, right?"

"Of course, it is. They are almost delusionally happy right now. That will settle down into a comfortable state soon enough."

Even Tina had to laugh over Angela's words. "Fair enough. And if not, then Rachel has us to help her through it, anyway, right?"

Angela just laughed and shook her head.

"I suppose you need to get back to your critters, and I ought to get home before mine start coming back."

"I always wished I could be at home when Tyler arrives from school. I think I miss out on learning so much about his day. By the time I get him he has unwound from it, which is good in a lot of ways, but I feel like I would be able to know him even better if I was there."

"It is a unique time of the day, for sure. I can often tell just from looking at their face what the day was like, even if they don't want to tell me right away." Angela didn't say it in a gloating manner, just matter of fact, as though agreeing with Tina. "But your mom tells you, right?"

Tina shrugged and nodded. "Yeah, I think so, at least she does sometimes, but I worry."

"You're too good at that," Angela interjected with a small smile, making Tina shrug again.

"Perhaps. But I meant to say that I worry she might miss things, or she's too wrapped up in dad's decline to notice if Tyler might be a little off. Tyler is such a great kid, I think anything bothering him might be very subtle. And he's very conscious of his situation, like that my parents are older and really doing us a favor by keeping him. That's why it was such a surprise that he was so persistent about asking to be signed up with that program. And also, why I finally agreed."

"You'll get to meet the guy before they go off anywhere, though, right?"

Chapter Six

*M**eet the guy?** Tina recoiled at the thought that this was even a question. Of course, she'd meet the guy. Hadn't she already said so? She'd interrogate him, examine his background information, and probably borderline stalk him before he even gets to *meet* Tyler. But she hesitated to say any of that to her friend. For one thing, Tina wasn't sure how to say it without sounding like the monster most of the public thought she was. It was hard for her to fake being sweet at the best of times. When there was the least bit of a hint that Tyler might be at risk in any way, she could go full on beast mode within the blink of an eye.

But Angela was her friend, her best friend, possibly her only friend, if one didn't count Rachel and Rachel's neighbor Evie. Tina didn't always count Rachel and rarely counted Evelyn, but that was just evidence of her issues. Whatever the case, Tina didn't want to alienate her friend. So, she tried to breathe through her initial reaction to what was probably an innocent question.

"Yeah, I'll meet him," she finally said after a deep breath and a gulp to swallow all the words she thought about saying.

"I'm sorry, Tina, I'm not sure how my question was wrong, but I can see that it was."

"No, it's not you, as usual, it's me. I'm just having a hard time with the idea of it. But I promised Tyler I would try, so we might as well not talk about it anymore."

She had just done her best to dismiss the subject when Angela's attention was caught in an entirely different direction.

"Clark, hey, how's it going?"

"Good afternoon, Angela, nice to run into you. I wouldn't have expected to see you here."

The deep voice came from behind her. It sounded familiar, but Tina couldn't place it. The deep manliness of it sent a small shiver through her core that she tried to ignore and suppress all at the same time, praying no one noticed her reaction.

"Tina, I'm not sure, did you get to meet Clark at the wedding?"

With those words, Tina remembered the handsome man who possessed that delicious voice and wished the ground would open and swallow her. She hadn't changed out of her scrubs, her hair was in a messy ponytail, and the dab of makeup she had put on that morning was likely either worn off or smudged all over the place.

Not that it mattered. What did she care what he thought of her? Vile, handsome man. It almost hurt her eyes to look at him.

Tina turned her head in a semblance of politeness. "We did meet. How do you do?"

"It was Tina, right? We didn't get a chance to talk much at the wedding." His warm, pleasant smile and attentive glance flowed over her as his gaze took in her outfit, and he frowned. "Are you a nurse? I didn't notice there was a clinic in this plaza."

"That's right, I'm Tina. And no, I'm not a nurse." She didn't elaborate, but her friend was an over-sharer by nature, it would seem.

"Tina's a veterinarian. A doctor, not a nurse, to be specific," Angela said, amusement evident in her tone.

"Oh wow, that must be fascinating work."

"It is, actually, yes."

"It must be even more challenging than being a doctor for humans as most people can tell you what's wrong with them or at least their symptoms."

"That's true. Although, even though animals can't tell you with words, I would say they're far more honest about their health than a lot of people I know."

Clark's easy-going smile drooped into a frown. "What do you mean?"

Tina shrugged, already regretting her words. She was no good at small talk. "Like how many hamburgers do you eat, for example? Do you tell your doctor the actual number or do you round down with the excuse that you don't want to receive a lecture?"

"If you aren't a doctor, how would you know this?"

A puff of laughter surprised Tina on its way out of her throat. It was bold of him to challenge her statement. But she wasn't wrong. She might be a vet, but vets have to go to at least part of medical school before switching to the specifics of animal medicine. But she wouldn't bother telling him that part.

"I have started accompanying my father on his frequent doctor's visits," she finally said, which terminated the conversation quite effectively. That hadn't exactly been her intention, but Tina wasn't disappointed to see the ridiculously good-looking man take his leave.

"Well, it was nice to bump into you, Angela. Please say hi to your husband for me. I'm looking forward to our golf game next week."

"Nice to see you, Clark. We'll see you around," Angela said, always pleasant. They both waited until he was out of earshot to say anything to each other.

"You are the strangest female on earth," Angela said in a burst of laughter as soon as she must have thought it was safe to do so.

Tina folded her arms defensively. "Why do you say that?"

"That man is beautiful enough that even I notice, despite the athlete I have at home."

"Don't be so shallow," Tina said with a half-hearted scowl.

"I'm not being shallow. You barely even looked at him. In fact, it felt as though his good looks are an extra mark against him in your mind. It just doesn't make sense to me. Does it make sense to you?"

"Men that pretty think they are the best thing that happened to God's green earth. I don't tolerate that well."

"Clark didn't strike me as that sort," Angela said firmly. "And you didn't give him the time to show if he is or not." Angela, usually the sweetest, smiliest person Tina knew, which could be annoying if you didn't love her, actually frowned at Tina. "You hate judgmental people, but you really are one yourself."

"I know, why do you think I hate it so much in others?" Tina wasn't even trying to hide her judginess. What would be the point? It wasn't hideable. But she also wasn't wrong about handsome men. She had never met one who wasn't at least a little like that. It was even understandable, really. When you looked that good, everyone else catered to you. Humans were visual, just

51

like most sentient beings. Beauty might be in the eye of the beholder, but society formed your view of beauty from a young age to the point that collectively, most people appreciated the same or similar features and traits. And the beautiful people profited from this. It went to their heads. Karl had been gorgeous, and look where that had gotten her.

"Would you say my husband is a hottie?" Angela asked.

"We both say it all the time."

"But do you mean it? Do you believe my husband is attractive?"

Tina started to fidget. "Your husband is a good-looking man, but I've never found myself inappropriately attracted to him, Angela, you know that."

"I'm not asking about that. But if you agree that my husband is handsome, then do you also believe he's self-centered and egotistical like you usually think about anyone extra good looking?"

Tina opened her mouth to answer but then had no answer to give.

"I've known him since we were in college."

"One could argue he was even better looking then."

"We all were," Tina countered drily. "But he's aging well."

Angela ignored Tina's aside. "Exactly, we were all hot. So, were we all egomaniacs?"

Tina shrugged. "Probably."

Angela laughed a little and then sighed. "My point," she said with a roll of her eyes, "is that you are being ridiculous about Clark. Just because he's good looking doesn't mean there isn't a decent human under the surface. You should have been a little more open to being pleasant with him."

"Sorry, Ang. Were you wanting to keep him around? I should really get going anyway. I should have let him take my spot."

"Now you're being extra ridiculous. I would far rather visit with you, and well you know it. But if Tyler wants a man in his life so bad, maybe you should think about getting him one. Clark is single and seems very nice –"

"No." Tina interrupted whatever Angela was about to say.

She wasn't even going to entertain the topic. And her best friend ought to know that. Agitation began to simmer under her skin, but she tried not to ever be vicious with Angela.

Angela, having known her since childhood, knew the reaction that was starting even subtly. "You ought to at least think about being open to the possibility, Tina. Losing your husband so young shouldn't condemn you to a life of loneliness."

Tina swallowed hard to keep her anger within bounds. She stood up, hoping it looked natural. "I know you mean well, Angela, and so I appreciate the kindness you intend. But I'm not lonely. I've got Tyler. And you. And my folks. And my clinic. Which I need to get back to. As usual, with you the time flies by. Thanks for the visit. I'll talk to you soon."

She sounded choppy and probably a little bit crazy. But Tina couldn't help that and didn't even really care. She just needed to get out of the coffee shop without exploding. She craved a pint of ice cream and an industrial-sized bag of potato chips right in that moment. There weren't enough self-affirming quips and quotes in the world to settle her feelings of anger and betrayal.

Deep breath in, hold for four, out for four, in for four.
She was going to hyperventilate if she didn't slow down
her breathing, but the usual exercise wasn't going to
cut it. She wanted to scream in rage and also sob with
despair. Life totally sucked when even your best friend
didn't understand your feelings.

Of course, if she had ever been fully honest with
Angela, she probably would understand. But Tina had
never told a single soul about certain aspects of Karl's
death. Well, everyone knew he was dead, of course. But
not some of the more sordid details surrounding why
he was where he was when he died in that car accident.

And she would *never* tell.

Tyler needed to believe his father had wanted him.
Tina would never inflict the truth upon her precious
son.

It was Karl's loss.

Sadly, Karl's idiocy had cost Tyler a father. But it
probably would have been worse for Tyler if Karl had
lived. Imagine the life they'd have had with a deadbeat
dad. There hadn't been much insurance, but it had at
least paid for the funeral and a few initial expenses in
preparing for Tyler's arrival. It didn't put a dent in the
student loans they had consolidated. So, Tina had been
saddled with paying for both of their educations. But
she was free of the man.

Not really free, if she was honest with herself despite
the simmering anger she was trying to quell. She
carried the baggage of her relationship with him every
single day. The physical marks hadn't lasted long but
the emotional burdens were with her forever.

But she had Tyler as recompense and that was
worth anything.

So, she would take her dark and twisted self back
under control and carry on as best she could. She

would find a most excellent seltzer-based drink of some sort that would taste excellent but would have few calories and she would bring it to Angela's house and apologize for being a jerk one day soon.

Thinking about Tyler had the usual effect of centering Tina back into what was truly important. It was the full explanation of why she felt misunderstood and was also the reason that was completely ok. The breathing and affirmations would work now. And then she would be immersed in cat dander and puppy fur for the rest of the afternoon. Who could be grumpy after that?

Tina could be, that's who. The thought brought a slight smile to her face as she helped her assistant clean up at the end of the day. She was tired and her back ached. One more reason to get herself more physically fit. Surely, she would be better able to take a busy day if there were less of her to haul around and her muscles were stronger.

"Thanks Ashley, you were great today."

"I appreciate that, Doctor Tina."

The young woman had been working with Tina for a few weeks now and seemed to be a reasonably good fit. She was a little annoyingly cheerful, but Tina couldn't hold that against her. She had probably been that way when she was Ashley's age. It didn't last.

"Have you thought anymore about taking some courses toward your technician's certification?" Tina asked as conversation. She wasn't trying to make a point and she didn't want to be forced to decide between hiring someone else or paying Ashley more at this point. But she did want to see into the girl's head.

Sadly, Ashley took it as criticism.

"I'm sorry, Doctor Tina, but I have no time or interest in tying myself up into student loans for the rest of my life. I will work hard for you, but you have to take me as is. If you can't, I'll have to look elsewhere." The bubbly girl said the words calmly and with such determination that Tina wanted to laugh, but even she wasn't such a jerk as to do so.

"I'm sorry, too, Ashley, if my question made you think I was somehow criticizing you or something. I wasn't. I was being honest with you when I said you were doing a great job. While it's true there will be some things that, by law, I can't have you assist me with if you aren't certified, for the most part, I'm thrilled to have your help and not have to pay you the big bucks."

Ashley laughed and relaxed. "Thank you, Doctor. I am really enjoying this job. The work is so fascinating and while you might not think you're paying me the big bucks, it's more than I've been able to get elsewhere, so I appreciate it very much. I won't let you down, I promise."

Tina wasn't sure how to take the young woman's earnestness. It was disconcerting and made her feel like she ought to be old and mature. She supposed she was getting there but aside from Tyler proudly announcing his own advancing years, it was easy for her to forget that she was thirty-four years old. Where had the time gone?

With a few more polite pleasantries exchanged, Tina left Ashley in charge of the clinic until the overnight minder arrived. Since they had performed three operations that day and were keeping two of their patients overnight, Doug would be staying with the animals in case of anything of concern. It cost Tina money but saved her so much stress and time that she was able to spend with Tyler, so it was worth it.

Chapter Seven

But where *had* the time gone?

Tina pondered that thought as she drove toward her parents' comfortable home to collect Tyler. Her mom had already called to ask if they would stay for supper, so Tina had a pretty good idea they would be asking her to help them with something. She didn't mind. It was a relief that they would ask her now. She used to have to try to pay attention and notice what needed to be done, and that was too stressful and hard. This way, if they could just tell her, it saved them a lot of time and worry.

But that still didn't leave her with a sense of satisfaction about where her life had gone. And yet she ought to be satisfied. She had built a reasonably successful business from scratch. She had finally paid off both her and Karl's student loans, and she was well on her way to having her house paid for. Tyler was awesome. Though she couldn't really claim that as one of her successes. She had been hugely blessed. She tried, of course, but with all her own failings, it was nothing short of a miracle that Tyler was so amazing. She supposed she could count it as a success that she hadn't ruined him. Or killed him when she was a young, grieving widow trying to finish up her internship and survive that terrible period in their lives.

Not that she had really grieved for Karl.

It was more that she had grieved the loss of what should have been. They had been so happy when they'd first started going together. They had both been very young and idealistic. She supposed now, in hindsight you could say they had been terribly naïve and immature, but Tina had believed they were deeply in love. So, they had wed. It was the biggest decision in both of their young lives, and they had been thrilled with it at the time. She had thought they'd be together forever.

But Karl had changed. Somewhere between their third and fourth years of college he had turned dark and bitter. Much like Tina was now but for quite different reasons in her unprofessional opinion. In hindsight, Tina was reasonably sure he was suffering from undiagnosed depression or some other mental or emotional problem that she had not been equipped at the time to deal with. And he had refused to seek help. She had suggested he see a doctor. Since she had taken many pre-med courses in preparation for veterinary school, she had known enough to recommend that. But he had refused, becoming angry if she would ever bring it up.

He had only actually hit her that one time. It had been enough to scare them both. But Tina had often wished he would hit her rather than use such cutting words with her. He was always sorry after and would treat her much better for a while. But then it would happen again.

Again in hindsight, Tina often thought she should have left him. But then she wouldn't have Tyler. Her precious son was the reason Karl had finally left *her*, but no one need ever know that nasty little tidbit of information.

Now, nearly eleven years had passed. The final remnants of their life together, aside from Tyler, were finally gone and dealt with. This, besides the health scare, was why Tina was doing her best to make a change. She had lived under the shadow Karl left over her life long enough. It was time for her to shed the unhealthy coping mechanisms along with the debt.

She was probably just as bad as Karl had always been for refusing to seek professional help. Reading books and repeating mantras likely wasn't going to heal what was broken within her. But she was ashamed of where she had allowed herself to go within her own neuroses. She didn't want to lay that all out for a professional to assess. That made her a coward of the first order. And perhaps a fool.

Tapping the steering wheel at one of the few traffic lights between her clinic and her parents' house, Tina thought about what she wanted to accomplish.

"You have a year," she told herself out loud, not caring if she was crazy for doing so. "One year from today. If you haven't managed to turn it all around for yourself in that time, you have to see both a medical and a psychological doctor for professional help. Because you'll surely need both."

Saying it out loud carried all the more weight in Tina's mind. She was committed. For Tyler's sake. Especially as he became a teenager, she needed to make sure she was on top of her game physically and mentally to be able to help him stay there, too. And she would be in a better position to keep up with him if she were healthy.

She still didn't need a man, no matter what Angela might think.

But other than that, she would try to be normal.

What was normal anyway? Pondering that conundrum accompanied her the rest of the drive to collect Tyler.

"Dad has to see a specialist off the island."

The way her mom said it, in a whisper, as though it were a vile secret, made Tina nervous.

"All the specialists are off island," she pointed out as reasonably as she could, trying to keep everyone calm. "When is the appointment?"

"We don't know yet. But you'll take us, right?"

Tina had to smile. They needed a commitment without giving her the information. But of course, she would take them. It didn't really matter when it was, she would be there. But she hoped it wasn't too last minute. She did have her own patients to consider. While it was true that they weren't human patients, their health certainly mattered to their human family members. But of course, she would take her parents to her dad's appointment. There was no question of that.

"Depending on which day of the week it is, maybe we could make a trip out of it and stay in the city for a couple days. We haven't done that in years."

"Oh no, your dad doesn't like the city."

"Speak for yourself, Lydia," Tina's dad finally piped up. "None of us have taken a vacation in longer than we can remember. That sounds like a good idea, Tina, girl," he added with a wink.

If he could talk of vacations, perhaps his appointment wasn't so serious. Or maybe he was dying and wanted to make the most of the time he had left. The lovely casserole her mother had made started to curdle in Tina's stomach, and she had to swallow hard to keep everything where it was supposed to be. There was no fear of her overeating tonight, she thought with snide amusement.

"Just keep me in the loop as early as possible so I can make sure any planned surgeries and such in my clinic are scheduled appropriately."

"Your father is more important than puppies, Tina," Lydia said sternly.

"I know that quite intensely, Mom," she said as patiently as she could. "But there's no need to inconvenience my patients unnecessarily. I'm sure your appointment will be scheduled with at least some notice, which I can pass on to my own appointments. If it ends up being last minute, we'll deal with that, but if I don't have to lose business over it, wouldn't that be better for everyone?"

Lydia harrumphed in a way that put Tina's teeth on edge. She tried to be understanding. Her mother was probably deeply stressed about whatever the doctor's appointment was for. And it was obvious this was going to be the center of their lives until it was sorted out. But it was also clear to Tina where some of her own acerbic side came from.

She really didn't want to be a harpy anymore. She needed to find healthier coping skills. Because that's all it really was – a way for her to protect herself from others. It sounded quite dreadful when thought out logically, but she supposed she had been subconsciously trying to hurt others rather than being hurt herself. That had to stop now. Especially while dealing with her parents.

"I swear, Mom, whenever the appointment is, I'll take you and we'll have as good a time as we can muster, whatever the doctor has to say. Never mind about my clinic."

"Don't be silly, Tina, girl. We'll tell you as soon as we know anything. While your patients might just be critters, they matter too."

Her dad was the best. Tina sternly ordered her eyes not to mist over at the thought there might be something wrong with him. Her family wasn't the best at communication. If they weren't sharing the concerns, she wasn't sure if she should ask. But that was quite stupid. They should turn that around along with everything else she was trying to change. It wasn't a pattern she wanted to continue with her own little family. She took a deep breath.

"What exactly are your doctor's concerns?"

"It's a geriatrician," Dad said while Lydia made a sound of protest. Dad looked at his wife. "She'll have to know sooner or later. It can't possibly be a surprise that we're aging, Lydia."

Out of deference to her mother's obvious wish to not talk about it, Tina did her best not to pepper her father with questions. She didn't know very much about that speciality. "Isn't Geriatrician kind of like a Pediatrician for kids? Like they just treat older people but it's quite a broad field of medicine?"

Dad nodded while Lydia remained silent. "There are just a few things they're worried about that might be related to my age. Some of them are mobility related and some are memory things."

Tina frowned. "Have you noticed decline in those areas? You seem the same as always to me."

"Which is why you treat puppies and not old men," Lydia pointed out with a bit of a pout. Her first instinct was to poke back at her mother, but instead Tina laughed.

"You have a point, Mom." Tina turned back to her dad. "I'm glad you asked me to take you. I'd like to be there when you see the doctor."

Neither of her parents agreed to that, but they didn't deny her outright either. Tina would leave the issue to another day. For now, she was finished with the meal, and it was time to get her son home. Her son, who had been quieter than usual throughout the meal.

Tina was determined to change all the patterns in her life despite the fact that the books say you should only try to change one bad habit at a time. Communication was one of those patterns.

"You didn't have very much to say over supper tonight, Ty. Everything okay?"

Tyler shrugged. Not a helpful reaction.

"Did something happen at school or at Grammy and Grampy's house?"

"No," he said in a small voice.

Tina felt a sudden urge to shake the usually cooperative kid but restrained the ridiculous impulse, lowering her voice and softening her tone. "I can tell something is bothering you, Tyler, but I can understand that you might not yet be ready to tell me about it. I would appreciate it if you wanted to share your thoughts with me. Please know that I'm here to listen when you're ready."

She didn't roll her eyes over the new-agey sounding words. Even if they sounded out of character for her, she really meant them. And she didn't want to force her son to share his thoughts. She was reasonably sure he would tell her eventually. Forcing him would probably damage his trust in her and make future sharing even more difficult. But it was so hard to be patient.

Thankfully, her patience was rewarded sooner than she expected.

"Why is everyone sick? Is Grampy going to die like my dad did?"

Tina blinked. She should have anticipated this. Her parents maybe should have as well and not brought up the specialist at the table. Tyler wasn't so young anymore that he didn't understand or notice such things.

"Oh Tyler, I'm sorry. That was insensitive of us to discuss over supper, wasn't it? I found it spoiled my appetite, too." She sighed and reached a hand over to pat his leg while still keeping her eyes on the road. "I don't have answers for you yet, I'm afraid. We'll know more when we see this doctor. Grammy and Grampy didn't even tell me what the doctor is looking for, so I'm not sure if we have to be really worried or not. So, I'm choosing not to worry until I know more. I hope you'll make that same choice."

"But how can you choose your worries? I'm worried now."

"I know, son, and I'm sorry. I probably have more practice on setting my worries aside than you do." She stopped for a moment to think. "It isn't so easy to choose not to worry, but let's think it through. Did Grampy look sick?"

"I don't think so."

"Has he seemed different lately than you can remember him being?"

"Not really. He still beats me at checkers, and he still can't throw a football."

Tina grinned at her son's choice of assessors. "So, from those things, it seems like he's fine, right?"

Tyler nodded.

"I'm not sure if this is the case, I'm just thinking out loud, but maybe it's possible that it's an automatic thing due to his age. Because the doctor they're going to see isn't super specific. Like an oncologist is for cancer and a rheumatologist is for arthritis, but geriatrics is a much broader specialty from what I can remember from my few medical classes."

"So, you don't think there's anything to worry about?"

Tina bit her lip. She didn't want her son worrying, but she wanted to have open and honest communication with him. "That's just it and why I think we should try not to worry. There are too many possibilities to know what to worry about, and it won't help us. Sometimes worrying can be productive. Like if you have a problem and thinking it through a lot can help you find the solution. But with this we don't even know if there is a problem, so worrying is just going to make us sick and not help Grampy at all."

Tyler nodded but still appeared concerned.

"Tell me what in particular you are worried about."

"I already don't have a dad. I don't want to lose my Grampy, too." Tina could hear the threat of tears in her son's voice and wished she wasn't behind the wheel so she could pull him into a hug. But she did grab his hand and hold on to it tight. Her own throat felt thick with unshed tears, and she had to clear it roughly to be able to speak.

"I can understand that thought and I fully agree. But like you said, he doesn't seem even the least bit sick, so I really don't think this is a matter of dying. I think that would be a different doctor, to be honest. I was happy to hear you say that Grampy still beats you at checkers because sometimes when people get older their mind weakens a little bit. Or their muscles, too. I think that's what a geriatrician looks after."

"That's still bad, though, right?" Tyler asked, his voice still small but sounding a little less deflated.

"It could be, but we really won't know until after he's seen the doctor. And we don't even know when that is. So, if you can, try to put it out of your mind for now and just enjoy every minute you spend with him. We'll know better what exactly we have to worry about then."

Even to her ears, this sounded part reasonable and part ridiculous. But thankfully Tyler nodded and from what she could see from the corner of her eyes relaxed back into his seat.

"I would also advise you to try not to worry about any of the adults in your life, Tyler. I know it seems all of a sudden everyone is having health problems, since I have had to alter our diet and now Grampy has this appointment. But this really doesn't mean any of us are near dying. Certainly not me and I'm pretty sure not Grampy, either. So, you will only be burdening yourself if you start obsessing over our health."

Tyler kept his gaze out the side window, but Tina could see the movement of his nod from the corner of her eye.

"I just wish my dad never died."

"I know, hun. I'm sorry for that."

Tina swallowed the acrid taste of lying. She wasn't actually sorry. At least not sorry that Karl wasn't in Tyler's life. She was nearly completely certain that Karl's presence in their lives would have been even more damaging to Tyler than not having a father. At least there was an explanation for his absence. An absentee father would leave a different kind of scar on the child's psyche, Tina was sure, even without a professional opinion. Besides how damaging it would be to hear his parents fighting or whatever might have been involved in their marriage or separation. Tina would never know if Karl would have come back after he left in a huff as though her pregnancy were completely her fault. But being with him had been no picnic before he'd left that day.

"At least I'm soon going to have a Big Brother, right?" Tyler asked eagerly.

"That you are," she agreed with as much cheer as she could muster. "Remind me to call your school tomorrow and I'll check on that for you."

"Would you?" Tyler asked eagerly, almost fully restored to his usual good cheer. "That would be awesome! Thanks Mom!"

Chapter Eight

Tina stared at her phone, hesitant to dial. She had promised her son she would call the school, so she had to do it. But the thought was curdling her stomach. Taking a deep breath, she punched in the numbers.

"Cape Avalon Elementary, how can I help you?"

"Good morning, this is Tina Archer, Tyler's mom. I'm calling about the Big Brother program you're organizing. We submitted Tyler's application on Monday."

"Yes, you were quite late putting that in."

"Right. Will that hold Tyler back from getting matched?" Tina was torn between hope and disappointment. She didn't want to hinder Tyler in any way but still...

"I want to tell you yes, just as a matter of course to teach you not to be so tardy," the secretary who'd answered the phone told her, surprising a puff of laughter out of Tina. "But I don't want to take out my irritation with your lateness upon your son. And the fact is, with only his application to deal with, there shouldn't be any delays at all."

Tina wanted to tell the woman what she could do with her opinions, but she too didn't want to interfere with Tyler's chances. "When should we expect to hear something? I'd like to meet the guy before he has any dealings with Tyler."

"Of course. Let me call you back this afternoon. I should have everything arranged by then."

"I appreciate it," Tina said as pleasantly as she could muster. "And I'm sorry we, or rather I, was late submitting. Thank you for not allowing that to hinder the arrangements."

"I'm sure Tyler will benefit from the program," the secretary said before disconnecting, leaving Tina to stare at her phone in surprise before another laugh was forced from her.

Stomach acid churned within her midsection making her reconsider the coffee she was about to pour. She hated meeting new people if they weren't the owners of one of her patients. And the thought of having to interview this individual with the intention of allowing Tyler to go off with him made her inclined to vomit the small breakfast she had already eaten.

Tina shook her shoulders and torso in an attempt to dislodge the tension accumulating there. She had animals to see to that required her full attention, and they would not react well to her being uptight. She did a little jog and dance in place to try to loosen herself. She should have waited to call the school on her lunch break. But she had promised Tyler.

Shaking her head, Tina tried to readjust her focus. The animals were waiting on her. With a deep breath, she put the issue from her mind for the time being. There was a pregnant cat that needed her undivided attention.

By two o'clock Tina had exhaustion fuzzing the edges of her consciousness and she realized she had worked through lunch, so she excused herself from the clinic to rectify that situation and to take a walk in the warmth of the day.

Deep breaths helped to loosen the tension that was again accumulating along her shoulder blades and neck. She nibbled on a cheese string as she strolled. It wasn't so dreadful trying to be healthy, she reflected even as her nose twitched from the smell of hot grease that came from the fast food joint not far from her clinic.

Turning on her heel, Tina diverted her route to avoid the temptation. She was determined to stick to the plan. According to everything she'd read, she might be able to divert her cravings if she behaved herself for at least three weeks. Tina didn't know if she believed that. French fries were always going to be her weakness, she was reasonably sure. But the dropping numbers on the bathroom scale were sufficiently satisfying to keep her motivated, at least for now. That and Tyler's fears of losing his family members. She would get follow-up blood work done in a couple months to see if her changes were doing any good.

She was determined to demonstrate healthy habits for her son to emulate. It wasn't too late for him. It wasn't too late for her, either, in most ways. But she was hoping Tyler was young enough that she could retrain his impulses or cravings so that when he was grown, he would crave fruit or something when a snack attack struck him rather than the rubbish she craved whenever she wasn't being careful.

The ring of her phone interrupted her less-than-helpful thoughts, which was a relief at first, but when she saw that it was the school calling she was reluctant to answer.

Finally, she did.

"I've got the information for you, Doctor Archer. And I've spoken with the Big Brother. He's a little bit older than most of the young men who sign up to the program, but I think he will be a good match for Tyler. He seems very pleasant and eager to get started. I'm just emailing you with his information right now."

Tina swallowed the bile threatening her esophagus and made the appropriate response. At least she hoped she did as she couldn't hear what the secretary was saying over the buzzing in her ears.

Clark Spencer

Tina frowned as she read the email. Why did that name seem familiar?

Her eyes widened as she remembered. He's Angela's friend. And he was a guest at Rachel and Jake's wedding. Had he arranged to be matched with Tyler? Should she be even more concerned than she had been? Was Tyler at even greater risk from this guy than he would have been from a stranger?

She wanted to cuss. She wanted a bag of chips. She wanted a real dad for her son or at least an uncle or something. Why had she been born an only child? If she had a brother, perhaps he could have filled this role for Tyler rather than them needing to seek this sort of help from a stranger.

What kind of man signed up for this sort of program? He was probably a big loser. Or worse.

Tina forced herself to take some very deep breaths. It was beyond her in that moment to do the proper breathing exercises she had started doing lately. But just breathing deeply helped her get centered again and prevented her from completely freaking out.

Somehow, she seemed to have terminated the phone conversation. Tina didn't think she had hung up on the other woman, but it was a possibility. Whatever had happened, it had been through automatic actions, not conscious thought. She did her best to calm down enough for actual thought.

She returned to the email and read the details in the background check. He had no criminal record. He had decent credit. He had moved around a fair bit, but she shouldn't hold that against him. His recent employment history included a couple months working for Jake. Tina could ask Jake privately about his impressions of the man. It might be a weird conversation, but Tina was willing to walk on broken glass or through fire or whatever for her son, she could bear up under one awkward conversation. Well, there would have to be multiple awkward conversations, she supposed. If she was going to confront the man himself, she couldn't imagine that being easy breezy either.

"Hello."

"Rachel? It's Tina, how are you?"

"Tina! What a nice surprise. I'm great, thank you. We're just about to get on the ferry back to the Cape."

"Oh no, Rachel, I'm so sorry, I forgot about your honeymoon. I'll let you go!"

"No, no, don't! I love Jake immensely, of course, but I've missed girl time. What's up?"

"Well, is Jake with you?"

"Yes, he's driving."

Tina hesitated for a second but then realized she could get two of her awkward conversations over at once.

"I actually wanted to talk to each of you. Or both of you, really. So, if you truly don't mind, this is actually really great for me. It's about Clark Spencer."

"Oooh! This is going to be interesting," Rachel said with a laugh. "Did you enjoy meeting him at the wedding?"

"Not particularly, that's not the sort of asking about I had in mind," Tina answered immediately and very drily, trying to keep the snark from her voice.

Rachel laughed again. "Just a sec, let me put you on speaker so Jake can get involved, then." There was a muffled sound of movement and Rachel telling Jake that it was Tina on the phone.

"Hi Tina, how's it going? Everything ok with you and Tyler?"

Tina appreciated that about Jake. He could be relied upon to get to the point and express concern.

"Yes. Or rather I hope so. That's why I'm calling. Maybe we ought to have this conversation in person. But let me tell you what it's about, and you can tell me if you are interested or willing to talk to me about it." She paused for breath while they made sounds of agreement and curiosity.

"So, Tyler has been begging me for at least a month to sign him up to this Big Brother-type arrangement his school is coordinating where the kids of single parents can get paired up with an adult for what should be a mentor-type relationship. In theory it sounds great, right? Tyler has been dying for lack of a man to play sports with and do things like camping and such. But the thought of sending him off with a stranger doesn't sit well with me."

"I'm sorry, Tina, I should have been more conscious of doing stuff like that with him."

Tina opened her mouth with surprise and shook her head but remembered they couldn't see her. "No, no, Jake, this is definitely not on you. And that certainly isn't the point of my phone call. You have a lot going on and just got married. And the program has supposedly found men and women who, and I quote "feel they have a child-sized hole in their lives." You've got your nieces and who knows, maybe you'll have a little blob of your own on the way."

Tina heard giggles in the background and tried her best to stay on topic.

"Anyhow. Tyler has been matched with Clark, to get straight to the point."

"So, you agreed?" Rachel demanded. "I'm so proud of you, Tina. I know that must have nearly killed you."

"I'm still in the dying stage, to be frank."

"Clark is a great guy, Tina," Jake interjected before Rachel could sidetrack the conversation again. "I haven't actually seen him around children very much. He's met my nieces, and they really took to him, which I take as a great sign. But I've found him to be very reliable, dependable, and trustworthy, which are probably qualities that you'd look for in someone you are entrusting your son with."

"And no skeezy tendencies that you've noticed?"

"Well, I don't always enjoy his choice of radio station on the job site, but that's the worst thing I can say about him. He's one of the good guys. I've often wondered why he doesn't have a family of his own. So, there's probably a backstory there of some sort. But from what we know of him, he's a great guy, and I would vouch for him. I'd even trust him with my nieces, so that's saying something."

Tina felt some of the tension leave her neck. "That *is* saying something, Jake, thank you. And again, I'm sorry to interrupt you guys. But thank you both for taking the time to talk with me."

"Hey, Tina, do you want us to arrange an evening where you could interrogate him without it being an interrogation? Like we could have you both over for dinner by coincidence?"

"Thanks, Rachel, that's kind of you. But I'd rather the interrogation be open and honest," Tina decided with a laugh.

"That's good of you, Tina. Promise you'll come over for a glass of wine after?"

"Absolutely," Tina agreed, even though she suspected wine should be on her list of restrictions if she was serious about her health journey. But this circumstance called for an exception. "Thanks, you guys, and again, I'm sorry for interrupting your honeymoon homecoming."

"We aren't teenagers, we'll survive the interruption," Jake answered with a deep chuckle as Rachel insisted, "Don't be a stranger, Tina. I'm overdue for some girl time."

Tina hung up feeling slightly better on a number of counts. For one thing, hearing her two newlywed friends sounding so happy and upbeat was reassuring. Perhaps the fact that they were well over twenty-one would help them to have a successful, happy partnership. She certainly hoped so, for their sake. And even for her own. If she wanted to remain friends with them, it would be better for her if they weren't going through a trauma or crisis. Not to make it all about her, she thought with a wry twist of her lips.

All right. Clark had been vouched for by people she trusted. Not that Jake or Rachel had known him for years, but they had known him much longer than she had. And if Jake said he'd trust the man with his nieces, perhaps she could consider entrusting Tyler to him. He wasn't a complete stranger anymore. Now it was time to speak with the man himself.

"Hello?"

Tina had to smile at the grumpy tone with which he answered the phone. She probably sounded similar when she answered an unknown number calling.

"Good afternoon, this is Doctor Tina Archer. We met briefly at Rachel and Jake's wedding. And then again at the Mocha Java when I was with my friend Angela? I'm Tyler's mom. He's a student at Cape Avalon Elementary?"

She stopped and took a deep breath wanting to kick herself for sounding so tentative. She was saying nearly every sentence like a question, as though she were asking him instead of telling him. She did not sound the least bit professional, and it was making her more angry than usual.

"I remember you, what can I do for you?" His tone had warmed considerably from his initial greeting. He now sounded like a bowl of chocolate pudding or a piece of fudge. Which was a completely ridiculous thought. But his voice was deep and low, and the pace of his words led her to think he might be from the south where life was more relaxed. She couldn't relate, but she kind of liked it. Not that she liked him. He was too handsome and self-assured for her to be the least bit comfortable around him. But that didn't matter in the least if he was going to be good to her son.

"Did you hear from the school?"

"Oh, Tyler's mom, I get it now." He said it as though he had thought she was calling him for a different reason, and heat filled Tina's chest with embarrassment.

Did he think she was calling him, calling him?? The thought mortified Tina. As if she would randomly call some guy she had met at a wedding. When he hadn't even given her his number.

She cleared her throat to be able to speak around the clog of anger and humiliation.

"So, your background check looks reasonable," she said as coolly as she could, hoping she sounded professional and calm. "I would like to meet to discuss

Tyler and understand a little bit more about you before I let you meet him."

"Of course, I guess it seems a little scary for you to let him go with someone you don't know, doesn't it?" She softened a little at his understanding of the situation. "I could have my mom call you, if that would make you feel better. Or my boss. Actually, you know my boss, so you could ask him."

"I already did, as a matter of fact."

"Oh." Clark sounded a little deflated.

"He was one of your references and the only one I knew, so I called him first."

"Of course. I can still give you my mother's number. She would be thrilled to hear from you, I'm sure."

Tina had to laugh. "Ok, I'll call her. But I'm fairly certain even axe murderers have mothers who love them."

"You think I'm an axe murderer?" He sounded aghast and Tina had to chuckle again, much to her shock. How could she possibly find anything amusing at a time like this?

"I don't know a single thing about you except that you don't have a criminal record and you're currently working in construction. But you've moved around a lot. Maybe it's because there were bodies in your last place."

"Wow," he drawled. "And here I thought I had issues with trust. You take it to a whole other level, don't you?"

"Tyler's the best thing that ever happened to me, and I would have to kill you if anything happened to him."

"That would be your right, of course," Clark replied immediately. "And I suppose it isn't going to reassure you in the least to say that I would want you to kill me if I allowed anything to happen to him. But I swear to you that I am a decent human and am just looking to give back a little."

Chapter Nine

Tina laughed but there was no real amusement in it.

"Someone with nefarious intentions would likely say the same thing, wouldn't they?"

Silence followed her question for a heartbeat before his rich chuckle filled her ear, making her uncomfortable in a completely different way.

"How about I take you for coffee, and you can get to know me a little for yourself before I meet Tyler?"

That had been Tina's intention but suddenly it almost sounded like a date or something, and she wanted to refuse but couldn't.

"I would appreciate that," she said in a voice that sounded stiff even to her own ears, but she couldn't make herself care. They were talking about Tyler. She would do anything to protect her son. Including having a non-date coffee with a handsome man.

She was the most ridiculous female ever born, she was sure. Most women would be thrilled to have coffee with the swoony, swarthy construction worker. He likely didn't have much going on in his mind, though, Tina scoffed. As buff as he was, he probably spent all his time working out or swilling steroids or something.

Don't judge a book by its cover.

Wasn't that one of the affirmations she was supposed to be using? She would hate for people to take one look at her and think all she did was eat bonbons all day. It would be an understandable assumption if you only looked at her bulges or how winded she got from walking. Clark had bulges of a completely different sort, she thought with slight amusement when she remembered how tight his t-shirt had been over his biceps and pectorals.

Giving her head a shake, Tina realized she had allowed silence to stretch on the phone, and she was again swept with a wave of embarrassment.

"Would it be possible for you to get away during the day? I would rather Tyler not know about this until we've come to an agreement."

"Sure, I could meet you on my lunch break tomorrow," Clark responded right away. "Our current jobsite isn't very far from where I saw you with Angie. Is that convenient for you?"

Tina blinked over his diminutive use of Angela's name. She wasn't the sort who did that with certain names, but other people did it all the time. If she had studied psychology like Angela had, she might know what that said about each of them. But, she remembered with a sigh, she didn't so she had no idea what it said. She was fully aware, though, that she was a kook.

"It is, thanks. My clinic is in the same plaza. Is noon good for you?"

"Well, if you wouldn't mind, earlier would be better for me. We actually start work early in the mornings to beat the heat. Ten thirty or eleven would be perfect, if that doesn't mess with your day too much."

"The coffee shop might be quieter then anyway. I'll make it work."

"Great, thanks, Tina."

Tina clenched her teeth to prevent herself from correcting him to call her Doctor Archer or even Doctor Tina. That would make her even more ridiculous than she already was. She was relieved for her restraint. But she barely replied before terminating the call and standing in her office staring at her phone.

The entire interlude of talking to Rachel and Jake and then Clark probably hadn't taken much more than ten minutes, but Tina was exhausted as though she had run a marathon or dug a trench. After a couple of deep breaths, she managed to drag herself through the rest of her day, hoping to keep the information from Tyler and make it to her appointment with Clark as promised.

She did survive the evening and managed to not drown her feelings in junk food. Tyler helped her with the required chores that evening, including cooking and cleaning up from supper, so well that they had time to go for another bike ride before bedtime. They chose an easy route because Tina just knew she wouldn't be able to manage any hills with the state she was in, despite how she had been improving.

To her surprise and relief, though, she slept like a log despite her swirling anxieties and so awoke feeling fresh and able to face her day. The patient load at the clinic was lighter than expected and she arrived a minute early for her appointment with Clark.

He was already there waiting for her.

"You made it!" he called with a grin. "I was so nervous about meeting with you that I got here early to save the best seat."

His eagerness was both endearing and nerve-wracking. Why was he so eager? Should she just reject him outright? Tina lifted her chin, pulled back her shoulders, took a deep breath, and smiled lightly.

"It is the best table, thank you for getting it. If we can't come up with anything to say to one another, at least we have a great view."

Clark laughed as though she had been joking. She hadn't been. But it was fine. She would rather not offend the man who might be spending time with her son.

"What can I get for you? My treat," Clark said as he gestured toward the menu.

"A large, black, hot coffee, please."

"Really?" Clark said with eyebrows elevated. "I would have thought you'd have some complex order that I'd struggle to remember like half frappé extra foam something something."

Tina was torn between being offended and amused. "What about me made you think that?" She clenched her teeth over the urge to gesture toward her size. She was sure she didn't need to draw this beautiful man's attention toward her overlarge frame.

He shrugged. "Every girl I've met likes froofy drinks when they're out for coffee." He shook his head. "But this is perfect. I don't even need to write it down." He moved toward the waiting barista and placed their order. Tina had to laugh when it turned out that Clark's order was a little froofy after all.

"You were just projecting, weren't you?" she asked him with a slight laugh. "You were hoping I'd order something like that so you could just say you were matching with mine."

"I'm man enough to admit I like my foam," Clark countered with a wink that quickly sobered Tina's amusement.

She blew on her tea as a way of avoiding his gaze. "What made you sign up for the program at Tyler's school?" It was the one question she needed answered most. She didn't care about small talk. What sort of man would do so? If she could believe his answer, and if it was a good one, she would entrust her son to him. Her stomach clenched.

"I grew up without a dad, and I have two little brothers," Clark explained in an earnest tone, looking at her eagerly but Tina tried to avoid his gaze, not wanting to be distracted by the bright blue of his eyes and miss the content of his words. He continued. "Our dad walked out on us when I was ten. I felt like I had to be the man of the house for my brothers and my mom, even though I barely knew what that meant. Our dad hadn't been the best role model before he left. But I did my best. So did she, don't get me wrong. Our mom was amazing and did so much for us."

Clark shifted his face to look out at the rolling surf, clearly visible through the window their table was next to. "I think what saved us was our neighbors. No, I know it is what saved me. They were a childless couple, a little older than my mom. I later found out they had always wanted kids and hadn't been able to have any of their own. The husband took an interest in me and my brothers. He taught me how to do things like shovel the driveway and repair the fence, mow the lawn, that type of thing. But not only that, he took us camping and threw the ball around with us in the evenings. He was our hero. When I was a kid, I never thought about it being a sacrifice for him. Then when I got a bit older, I felt as though we had taken advantage of their kindness, always running to them for stuff and taking his time. But now that I'm even older, I realize that maybe we filled a hole they had in their lives, too, that it was a mutually beneficial arrangement in certain ways. Don't get me wrong, with the three of us right next door, I'm sure we were a bit much at times, but I'm now feeling like there's a missing piece in my life, and I would love to fill it by extending some of the same sort of time as our neighbor extended to me."

Tina stared at him. If the story was even mostly true, it was a pretty great one. She knew she was more skeptical than most people, but she didn't really care. Tyler was her priority. But Clark's explanation was a reasonable one for why a seemingly normal man would offer to spend time with a boy he didn't know. She could accept the concept of wanting to give back or pay it forward when something similar had been done for him in a similar situation.

"Do you still see your neighbor?" she thought to ask.

"Yeah, they still feel like our family. We don't have a lot of family, which was part of why we were on our own back then. Of course, it might have been mom's pride, too. She was embarrassed that her husband had walked out on her and didn't want to ask for help."

Tina nodded. "I can understand that."

Clark's grin was blinding. "Yeah, I can see you being the type who wouldn't ask for help." He laughed. "So does this completely gall you?"

Tina had to smile and nod. "It does a bit. But I'll do anything humanly possible and even attempt the impossible if needed for my son."

Clark nodded. "So, what's the problem?"

"I'm not certain it is humanly possible for a mother to sit back and allow her son to go off with a stranger. At least for your mom, she knew the neighbor."

Clark nodded along with her words. "I can see why you'd say that. But since your friends can vouch for me, that must be of some assistance, right?"

Tina shrugged. "Somewhat. That's why I agreed to meet with you." She paused and then added in what she tried to be a gentle voice but since she felt like screaming, she wasn't sure if she pulled it off. "I still feel like it's a massive risk."

"Is there anything I can do or say that would help you feel better about it?" Clark's frown appeared to be one of kind concern rather than censure, which made Tina feel like even more of a grouch than usual.

"I'm not sure if there's anything that will make me feel good about this, to be frank." A puff of laughter escaped her despite her turmoil. "What sort of things do you plan to do with Tyler?"

Clark shrugged. "It depends upon him, really. I don't know anything about him. I'll try to cater to his interests. It would be great if they align with mine, but if they don't, then I'll have some things to learn."

Tina blinked and some of her resistance melted. It was exactly the right thing to say. He probably would be interested in the same sorts of things, from the look of him. But the fact that he would be willing to adjust to Tyler's interests and needs endeared the man to her.

"That's good," she accepted. "But I'll have to come with you the first few times you spend with him. I hope you'll understand."

"Of course. I'm on probation."

"You are?" she asked, horrified, "That wasn't in your file."

Clark laughed and waved his hand, still relaxed despite her dismay. "No, no, not that kind of probation. I meant with you. You are reserving judgment. It's like if I was starting a new job. Sometimes it's up to three months where they can fire you for any reason during your probationary period."

"Ah, I see," Tina said, even as bile climbed up her throat. Not that people on true probation were lesser humans or something, but she just couldn't allow her son to spend time with a criminal.

Clark's rich chuckle was low, but it filled the space between them, not lessening Tina's discomfort in the least. "You still aren't feeling reassured, are you? I'm sorry. It was a poor choice of words under the circumstances." He blew out a slightly frustrated breath while running a restless hand through his hair. "I'm sorry, Doctor Tina. I didn't really put myself in your shoes. I never thought I would have to prove myself to be able to spend time with your son. But I probably should have. I suppose it was a bit presumptuous of me to think you'd be eager to send him off and get a break. If I was a parent, I can see how this could be an awkward situation." He furrowed his forehead and looked at her earnestly. "Is there anything I can do to set you at ease?"

Tina shook her head and felt the prickle of tears threatening, which made her angry. She didn't cry. She was not a weeper. She never had been, except when she was pregnant. She had reason to be then. Her husband had died, and she was young, pregnant, and not yet graduated. But now was not the time for tears. She took a deep breath, drew back her shoulders and lifted her chin. "No, I can't be at ease with this situation, I'm sorry to say. But I told Tyler I'd at least try my best. So, I will accompany the two of you and try to wrap my head around it. I'll also call your mother."

Clark laughed again. "She'll be thrilled to hear from you, I'm sure. Although, I have to warn you, there's a chance she'll try to convince you to marry me, but just ignore that. She does that with all of us."

Tina opened her mouth to reply but nothing came out.

"Don't worry, I'm sure you'll be able to handle her just fine."

Tina heard censure in his voice again, but she wasn't sure if she was imagining it or not.

"So, when can I meet Tyler?" Despite her hesitance, Clark still seemed eager to go forward with the arrangement. Tina couldn't decide if she was relieved or disappointed. Her stomach clenched further, but she did her best to ignore it.

"How does your weekend look? If Tyler gets any homework done on Friday, he'll be quite flexible the entire weekend."

"I don't want to force anything or make him uncomfortable," Clark began. "I'm a stranger for him, too. Do you have a suggestion?"

Tina found it *almost* endearing that he was asking her. Or rather, she supposed a normal woman would find it so. She just wanted to throw up her hands and reject this whole idea. But she had promised Tyler.

"The beach is always popular," she heard herself saying. "How do you feel about the beach? He'd love to throw a ball or go biking or swimming," she heard herself start to babble. "If you know how to skip rocks and could teach him, he'd be your friend for life." She wanted to cover her mouth to stop the speech from flowing. Why was she telling him all this? Did she *want* it to work out?

Well of course she did, on one hand. She couldn't argue the fact that Tyler needed someone to help him with the things he was interested in that she couldn't quite manage to take an interest in. She had done her best. She'd learned to make mud pies when he was little and all the other horrid things little boys loved. But she had her limits. And she was only one person. It wasn't fair to Tyler to make him more responsible than he needed to be at a young age. She didn't want him swallowing his disappointments any longer. She hated seeing the longing in his eyes when his school friends went off with their fathers.

If she could allow this to work, if she could trust this Clark person, it would be a great experience for Tyler. And since the guy actually seemed eager to have a youngster in his life, she could relax a little about his motivations. She wasn't imposing on him. She hadn't asked him to sign up for the program. If he wanted to do it, he wasn't even doing her a favor. She didn't have to feel as though she were burdening someone else with her responsibilities.

For the first time since Tyler had told her about his interest in the program, Tina felt herself relax, at least an increment. She would never be relaxed until she was dead, she doubted, but where it came to Tyler and this program, maybe she could see the bright side eventually.

"If the weather's good on Saturday, would that work? I don't want to seem too eager. Eight o'clock is probably too early, right?"

Tina actually allowed herself to laugh genuinely over his question. "Maybe a little," she said mildly. "The forecast is good, so unless it changes drastically, let's plan to meet at ten."

"You don't want me to pick you up?" He frowned.

"I don't need you to know where my son lives until I have decided I'm going to trust you."

Chapter Ten

C lark almost winced. He respected her protective stance about her son. Being a single mom had to be difficult, especially nowadays. His own mom seemed to have done just fine, but Clark suspected it was slightly easier twenty-five years ago. And then they had their awesome neighbors who happily took on some of the load. But here he was offering her the same thing. You'd think she'd be a little happier about it.

He tried to rein in his frustration. Why couldn't the school have connected him with someone all too eager to send their kid off for a time? That would have been easier for everyone. He hadn't anticipated the need to audition for the role he wanted to play in a boy's life.

He ought to have married and had kids of his own. That had always been his plan. But here he was rushing toward forty and still it felt like he had so little to show for it. A bank account full of cash wasn't going to keep him company when he was older. When he was in his twenties, he had thought amassing wealth was the most important thing he could do, motivated by feeling deprived as a boy. Now, in retrospect, he realized he hadn't really missed out on anything when he was a kid. Between his mom and the other two adults in his life, he'd had all that had mattered and then some.

But now he found he really wanted to be able to turn that attention and knowledge he'd gained to good use, trying to help another boy who had been on the same path he was. Why wasn't she letting him? He tamped down his frustrations.

Clark smiled as cheerily as he could. She was the boy's mom. She had all the power in this particular situation. He couldn't irritate her with the jokes he usually used to diffuse an uncomfortable situation. She had struck him as particularly humorless the previous times he'd met her.

"That makes sense in a completely cautious way. I can respect that," Clark finally answered. It was true. If you were totally paranoid, you wouldn't want anyone to know where you lived. On the other hand, he was pretty sure the boy and his mom's information was on the paperwork he had been given. Better not tell her that, though or she might have a coronary.

She actually looked like she might be a ticking time bomb in that regard. Poor thing. He hated to be completely superficial, but if she lost a little weight, she'd not only be even more gorgeous, she'd also have a far better quality of life. And she might be able to do the things her son was most interested in.

Clark clamped down on his frustration further, as best he could. Just because he was ready to get on with having a boy in his life didn't mean said boy's mother was ready to accept the situation, even if she did submit the application. Perhaps he should just ask the school for anther placement after all. But Clark had never been one to back down from a challenge. And with a mother as paranoid and mistrustful as this, Clark suspected the boy desperately needed someone more relaxed in his life.

Not that Clark fully considered himself relaxed, but he had come so far in his own life's journey. He was certainly far more relaxed than the woman nearly vibrating in front of him.

"Since the Cape is nearly completely surrounded by beaches, do you have a particular one you guys prefer?" Clark asked when the doctor in front of him continued to sit in silence, finally sipping on her tea.

That was an oddity in itself. Tea. Who drank tea in the middle of the day? That was going to send her into a nap, wouldn't it? Not that the anxious woman looked ready to fall asleep. Finally, Clark felt his compassion start to kick into gear. He couldn't imagine being as uptight as she evidently was. She looked like she wanted to cuss him out but was holding it back. Being that sour must curdle her blood every single day. Clark started to worry he wouldn't like her son.

But that was absurd. There wasn't a ten-year-old boy on the planet he couldn't like, he was sure. It was the perfect age to befriend a boy. He would still be full of childish curiosity with the burgeoning knowledge and widening understanding of things around him. Clark was eager to move along with the arrangement. And so, he needed to make sure the mother didn't die of a heart attack at the thought.

He kept his smile contained and even tried to restrict his gestures. He was probably too big for her liking, viewing him as a threat. But there wasn't much he could do about his six-foot-three frame and the way his body reacted to the hard manual labor he had been doing for the past few months.

Despite his healthy bank balance, he liked to keep busy, and he found the physical labor soothed some of his restlessness. Being out in the fresh salty air most days didn't hurt any either. He loved his new life on Cape Avalon and hoped to supplement it by filling the one hole he felt was left in his life – a child to help. Now that Clark's brothers were well along in their own lives, they were turning to him less and less for advice or help. Clark missed that. He needed that. He hoped Doctor Tina's boy would be the perfect antidote to that lack.

And so, he had to make sure he didn't scare the rigid woman off.

"We do have a favorite beach," she finally answered him, as though it had been a difficult question. "It's never overrun with tourists, so it's perfect. Are you familiar with Sugar Beach?"

"With a name like that, I'm surprised it's not overrun," he replied. "No, I haven't been there yet. Does it show up on Maps?"

She bit her lip, appearing uncertain about what she was about to say for the first time since they began their conversation. "I'm not sure. I've just been going there since I was a kid. It's not far from here. I can probably draw you a map if it doesn't show up on your app."

"No problem, let me check."

It did, in fact, show up on the app he used for getting around anywhere unfamiliar.

"So, I'll meet you and Tyler there at ten on Saturday?"

She nodded without enthusiasm but then surprised him with a smile that actually reached her eyes.

"Tyler is going to be thrilled." She said it with conviction but no pleasure. She leaned closer to him, and Clark was surprised by an uptick in his pulse. Objectively, she was pretty if you liked mama bears. He was leery of such creatures, himself. But he could understand his body's instinctive reaction. And then his blood turned to ice. "I have to just tell you, though, Clark, that if you hurt my son in any way, I will kill you.

And as a veterinarian, I have access to the means of doing so in such a way that I'm likely to not even be caught. So, you'd best watch yourself."

She said it with such a straight face that Clark took her at her word and felt a flutter of nerves in his stomach. He could take on any opponent; he felt confident in his own abilities. But he'd never fought a woman before. And he had enough knowledge of nature to know what mother bears were like. The woman might look only a little like one, but he was certain she could be as ferocious as one if called upon.

"I swear to you, I have every intention of treating your son well. I appreciate your taking the time to see me today, and I understand it's a great risk you're taking to allow me to see your son on the weekend. I will do my utmost not to violate that trust."

Her eyes narrowed at him as though to assess the validity of his words, but then she nodded as though she had accepted them. She stood suddenly and extended her hand to shake his.

Clark was surprised to feel tingles in his hand when it closed over her much smaller one. It would be the most ridiculous thing if he were to develop warm feelings for the snide woman before him. There was no reason for him to do so aside from the fact that he had to respect a woman who was willing to threaten anyone who put her child at risk.

"Could I also get your mother's phone number?" she asked politely before taking her leave.

Chapter Eleven

Tina had to rush to the bathroom as soon as she got back to the clinic. She threw up anything that had been consumed that morning. It was the worst sensation. She hated vomiting and almost never did it, so it was a testament to how very upset she was about the situation.

She was being ridiculous; she knew that. While it was completely rational to be overprotective, Tina was reasonably sure she was taking it about twenty steps too far. She had just threatened to kill the man and get away with it. What sort of lunatic would he think she was? Would he even show up on Saturday?

Tina couldn't even begin to imagine how she would explain it to Tyler if he were to find out that she had ruined his chances with a Big Brother.

She thought she was done being sick, but that thought brought another rush of convulsions in her stomach.

Tina rinsed her mouth and stared at herself in the small mirror over the sink, barely recognizing the wild-eyed woman who looked back. Should she call Clark and apologize? Would that make it better or worse? Should she just wait until Saturday and see if he showed up? If he did, she swore to herself, she would do her best to act like a rational member of the human race.

Perhaps she needed to find a therapist sooner than she had planned. She ought to have done it already, really. She had just been putting it off due to her own discomfort and not wanting to explain herself to anyone.

Who could she talk to?

Rachel's neighbor Evelyn might understand. She was desperate for children. She might understand being irrational about protecting the one you had. But she was also a super sweet woman who might be able to give her some guidance on acting normal.

She also wasn't really Tina's friend, so Tina might be able to get away with not telling her much. But did she even have Evelyn's phone number? She certainly couldn't ask Rachel for it. She also wasn't sure how she could show up at Evelyn's place without Rachel seeing her.

Tina sighed and checked her phone before another sigh escaped her, this time one of relief. She did have Evelyn's number from when they were planning a small shower for Rachel when they had gotten engaged. That was another time she had been borderline crazy. Evelyn would understand, Tina was certain.

"Hello?"

"Evelyn? This is Tina, Rachel's friend."

"Tina! How delightful to hear from you. How've you been? And that delightful little boy of yours?"

"I'm ok. I've been better, to be honest. That's why I'm calling."

"Oh, I'm sorry to hear. What can I do?"

Tina appreciated the woman's instant kindness. She didn't think she herself had ever been like that. She was always suspicious and guarded. At least since she'd been an adult, especially since becoming a widowed single mother. But she could learn some behaviors from this kind woman.

"This might sound weird, but I don't really want Rachel to know I'm talking to you."

Evelyn's gentle laugh came over the phone. "She's quite distracted at the moment, it shouldn't be hard to hide it."

"It won't make you uncomfortable? I know you're good friends."

"You're kind to worry, but if I can help you, I'm sure she would understand if she were to find out we were keeping secrets. So no, it won't make me uncomfortable. Tell me what I can do. Do you want to talk on the phone or meet for a coffee or a walk on the beach? What would make you more comfortable?"

Tina's laughter didn't hold mirth before she answered the other woman. "Nothing will make me comfortable, I'm afraid, but yes, talking in person would be best. A walk would be perfect, but I'm not sure when we'd have time."

"If you don't mind using your break from work, I could come to your office, and we could walk on the beach there. I know it's a little busy there but not so bad that we couldn't have a private conversation as we walked."

"You wouldn't mind?"

"Not at all. I'm excited you've reached out to me, and I'm eager to be of assistance."

Tina felt humbled by the other woman's kindness. She really could learn from her. She doubted she ever would, but she admired the woman's ability to be so kind despite the blows life had thrown her way.

"Would you have time tomorrow?"

"I have plenty of time. Do you want to set an appointment now or let me know tomorrow what time is best for you?"

"Thank you so much, Evelyn. Your availability and flexibility are such a kindness. Can we say tentatively eleven o'clock, and if it has to change for whatever reason, I'll text you tomorrow?"

"That's perfect. I'll see you then." She paused for a second. "And try not to obsess over whatever is bothering you. I'm sure we can figure out a way through it."

Tina swallowed the lump that formed as she disconnected the call. Just talking briefly with Evelyn had calmed her racing heart and thoughts. She felt a degree of hope for the first time in ages, and she actually looked forward to talking to the woman she had previously considered too flighty to be friends with.

Evelyn couldn't be too much older than Tina and her friends, but she sometimes acted like a granny with her frilly curtains and baked goods. Rachel had explained that she was quite desperate for children and her constant baking was her effort to fill the hole in her life. Tina felt a momentary qualm that she was being unkind to the woman to discuss Tyler with her. But she was too desperate for the assistance to call her back and retract her request. Tomorrow couldn't get here soon enough.

Somehow, Tina managed to survive the remainder of her workday and her roiling emotions despite Tyler's eagerness to discuss the possibilities of gaining a big brother. Tina still hadn't told him about their arrangements, but apparently there had been other recent matches arranged at the school and it was all he wanted to talk about.

"Jeff said he's going camping with his new friend and Lydia had gotten her nails done with hers. I think that's a stupid activity, but Lydia was really happy about it, so I guess that's the point, right?"

"You're probably right," Tina agreed, trying to swallow the bite of supper she had just taken. "I didn't realize there were so many kids in your school with single parents."

Tyler nodded vigorously. "I think I'm the last one to get matched, so it sounds like a lot, but according to our social studies teacher, it's within the average."

Tina was able to laugh over that tidbit of information. "I'm glad to know we fit into the parameters of normalcy."

Tyler only shrugged. "Do you think it's because my name starts with T?"

Tina frowned at him. "Do I think what is because of that?"

"Is that why I haven't gotten my Big Brother yet? Because I'm later in the alphabet?"

"It's possible, I suppose," Tina agreed as her stomach started to roil anew. "I'll call the school tomorrow and check on it, ok?"

"Thanks, Mom. I know you're worried about it, so I'm extra grateful that you're going along with it. I'd hate to find out I missed out because my application got lost in a pile of papers."

"That would be terrible," Tina said, trying not to roll her eyes. It would have been delightful. Except that she had already called the school as she had promised her son she would. And she knew who he had been matched with. And she had probably blown it for her son.

Rather than calling the school the next day, she would call Clark and verify if he was coming. Since today was Thursday, it was only the day after tomorrow they were supposed to meet. She could excuse her phone call as just confirming the time. Then he could tell her if he was going to renege on their agreement.

She would call after she talked to Evelyn. Maybe that would help her sound less like a lunatic.

Somehow Tina made it through the night and again slept well, despite her roiling thoughts and the overactive acid in her stomach. She was becoming increasingly convinced that being active was helping with her sleep as she and Tyler had again gone for a bike ride after they'd cleared up from supper.

"You look much less harried than you sounded on the phone yesterday," Evelyn greeted her with a laugh and a vanilla-scented hug. "I brought some cookies for Tyler. I hope that's ok. I remembered, after I'd prepared them, that Rachel mentioned you are trying to diet. So, if you'd rather I not give them to you, I'll understand."

Tina smiled even as she wondered if this sweet but struggling woman would be able to help her. She obviously had her own issues and insecurities. But she had come with the intention of helping her, so Tina couldn't change her mind at this point.

"I'm actually getting quite a bit better at self-control. And Tyler loves your cookies, so I'll take them with a big thank you. And I'll try my best not to indulge."

Evelyn's wide smile made Tina glad she hadn't refused them. She quickly dropped them off in her office and then the two set off for the boardwalk across the street.

"I appreciate your coming, Evelyn. I'm sure you had other things to do today."

"Not really. I was thrilled to have a reason to get out of the house," Evelyn admitted. "So don't for a second think you've inconvenienced me. I'm not certain I'll be able to help you, but I will definitely do my best."

Tina was grateful they were walking and therefore she wasn't forced to look into Evelyn's face with all that earnestness most likely displayed all over it. Tina wasn't sure what to do with it. If she didn't want the woman's help so desperately, she would probably say something sarcastic and cutting and be done with it. But she knew Evelyn was sincere in her sweetness so it shouldn't put Tina's teeth so on edge.

"I want you to give me some tips on being normal."

Evelyn laughed. "I'm not normal, so I don't know how I could do that."

Her response surprised a laugh out of Tina but before she could say anything, Evelyn continued.

"For normal you should have asked your friend Angela. I think she's the steadiest person I've met. Besides she studied psychology, didn't she?"

"She did, yes, and I can see what you're saying. No one is normal. What is normal, right? But I can't talk to Angela about this. She knows too many things and will put too many connections together that I'm not comfortable talking about right now. I just need some tips how to get through this particular situation."

Tina was grateful that the other woman didn't even appear to mind that Tina had no intention of sharing the details with her.

"Ok. Tell me what's going on and I'll try to help, as long as you understand that it might not be a normal response."

They both chuckled even though Tina's felt a little hysterical. She was losing her mind over this stupid situation and was being beyond ridiculous. Clark was just a man. He didn't have serial killer vibes and he didn't strike her as the sort who was going to abduct her son or worse. Not that she really knew what vibe that sort of person gave off, but he really seemed, for lack of a better word, "normal." But she had probably blown it with him and needed help.

"So, I have an issue or ten, as you've probably noticed. I won't delve into my reasons and back story, but I'm cranky and suspicious most of the time." Evelyn looked like she was about to protest so Tina held up her hand. "Don't object just to be sweet. I know it's true, and I'm ok with it most of the time. But I think it might have caused a problem this time. And it's an important matter. So, I need some suggestions on how to smooth the matter over."

"Ah, I see, all right. Tell me about the situation and maybe between the two of us, we can come up with something."

"Tyler's school has partnered with Big Brothers and is arranging matches for the children with less-than-ideal situations or those who really want them. Like boys with only one parent, for example. Tyler begged me to agree to let him join the program. I didn't want to. As a child of the eighties and nineties, I was raised on all the horrors that could happen to a child at the hand of strangers."

"I don't blame you for being cautious."

"But with the promise of background checks and all that, and with Tyler begging me nonstop, I agreed. And he was matched. With a guy who was at Rachel and Jake's wedding."

"Well, that's good, right? They can tell you whether or not you can trust him, right? So, he isn't a perfect stranger."

"Yeah, well, they did. But it wasn't enough to calm my fears, and I'm afraid I might have offended him when we met, and what if he doesn't show up for Tyler tomorrow? What will I tell Tyler? And the school?"

Anxiety and anger swirled in Tina's gut making her regret having eaten breakfast, but she managed to breathe through the nausea, and it settled somewhat while Evelyn contemplated what she had been told.

"I would think a man who would sign up for such a program and submit to the likely invasive sort of background check one would expect of such a program wouldn't be so easily turned off by a bit of parental resistance. What makes you think he might not show up? Did he indicate that in some way?"

"No, but I was pretty rude to him. I wouldn't show up if I was him."

Evelyn laughed. "Ok, that's fair, I suppose." She stopped again. "Did he tell you why he wants to be a Big Brother? That might tell you whether his motivation is strong enough to overcome the barrier you presented."

Tina nodded as she thought back to her conversation with Clark. "Yeah, he seemed pretty excited and almost invested in the concept of being involved in a boy's life. It's like a pay it forward type of situation for him, but even stronger than just a philosophy."

"There you go, so he isn't likely to give up so easily, is he?"

"No, but he could ask the program for a different match, couldn't he?"

"Maybe. What did the forms say? Could you ask for a different match if you didn't care for him?"

"Oh, that's a good question," Tina exclaimed. "Thanks Evelyn! The paperwork was fairly clear that you were to give it at least a good enough chance. That they had worked hard at matching appropriately and that you shouldn't just back out due to personality differences, at least not without giving it a good try. So, you're right. If he hasn't even met Tyler yet, he probably can't just ask for a switch, unless he was to tell them that I'm insane. But he probably would hesitate to do that since he works for my friend's husband." Tina sighed and laughed. "You've taken such a weight off my shoulders, Evelyn, thank you so much."

Evelyn laughed, too. "Well, I don't think I really did anything, but I'm glad that I could help out." They continued walking in silence for a few steps while the older woman thought the matter through a little further. "Since you were hoping for some advice, might I make a suggestion?"

"Of course, please," Tina said, even though she didn't usually appreciate advice. But Evelyn was right, she had asked, she needed to be willing to hear it.

"I know, as you said, you have your reasons for being suspicious, and I'm sure they're valid and at least somewhat reasonable. But the next time you see this man, especially, I think you said it's tomorrow that he's to meet Tyler?" At Tina's nod, Evelyn continued. "Try this, then. Listen more than you speak. Observe him. Don't jump in with any sort of commentary of your own. That will tell you what you need to know."

Tina wrinkled her nose and forehead as she thought about Evelyn's words, making the other woman laugh.

"I know, that will be a challenge for you but just try it, especially if you really think you might have offended the man. It will kill two birds with one stone. You will have greater insight into who you might be allowing your son to spend time with, and it will prevent you from saying anything you'll have to apologize for later."

"That will be hard. Sarcasm is my default setting."

"I know, but the fact that you called me tells me you're trying to reset that default. Was I wrong in thinking that?"

Tina sighed. "No. Not wrong." She sighed again. "But it's so hard. It has been my *modus operandi* for so long, I don't really know how to operate without it."

"I suspect Angela would say it's a defence mechanism."

Tina smiled. "She probably would."

"Well, I'm sorry for whatever you've been through that made you need it, but I'm glad that you must feel safe enough in your situation now to be willing to try to change it."

Tina blinked. Evelyn was right. Things had changed enough that she felt she had enough power not to have to prove it at every turn.

"You're a pretty smart lady, Evelyn. You're going to be a great mom."

Evelyn flushed a little but wouldn't quite meet Tina's gaze. Tina wished she hadn't made that last comment. She had meant it sincerely but knowing the topic was a sensitive one, she shouldn't have touched it. She sighed and reached out to touch the other woman's arm.

"I'm sorry, Evelyn. I'm still learning about sensitivity and other forms of speech than sarcasm. I didn't mean to nudge a touchy subject."

"No apology needed, and you're doing great if you've come so far as to realize and apologize all in one breath, good for you."

Tina laughed but there wasn't a great deal of amusement in it. Yeah, good for her. Things that teenagers learned. What she hoped Tyler was developing, she was just learning to do herself. Like think before she spoke and not offend others with her speech.

Maybe she was too old to learn. She was supposed to learn these things twenty years ago.

Tina shook her head to rid herself of the defeatist thinking. She was a grown woman. A successful grown woman. She had a successful, growing veterinary practice that she had started from scratch. She had a fantastic kid. She was getting her health under control. She was obviously far from stupid. If she couldn't learn to be genuine in her kindness toward others, she could at least learn to fake it, right?

That thought was just twisted enough to amuse her, and she was able to take her leave of Evelyn without finding herself in a depressive funk. She had her animals to get back to. That was the best part of her day. The animals were genuine. Yes, they might be cranky, but it was always for a real reason, one she could usually help them with.

At the end of the day, when she picked Tyler up from her parents' house, she reminded herself this was the true best part of her day. Seeing Tyler's joy at her arrival was the best reward a mother could receive.

She tried to listen with her full attention as he bubbled over with all the things he had experienced through the day. She was reasonably sure he wouldn't always be so willing to share all his thoughts and feelings with her. Angela had recommended books to her on how to communicate with teenagers. She had started reading them already in anticipation, but they made her anxious and fretful, so she had set them aside until she truly needed them. Thankfully Tyler was still willing to share freely.

Chapter Twelve

But she couldn't keep her mind focused fully on paying attention to Tyler as she normally would. Her mind kept shifting back to the conversation she had with Clark on the phone before picking Tyler up.

"Hello?"

His deep voice had sounded hesitant, as though he wasn't certain he wanted to even answer the phone. Tina couldn't blame him, considering their previous conversation.

"Hi, Clark? It's Tina calling about tomorrow," she'd said, hoping her tone was light and friendly and didn't reveal all the convoluted thoughts convulsing through her head.

"You aren't calling to cancel, are you, Doctor Tina?"

Tina closed her eyes and fought the various inappropriate reactions that were fighting with her nerves. It didn't matter that his deep voice reminded her of chocolate nor that she never spoke with men on the phone. Literally never. Except her father, maybe and even that was extremely rare as her mother claimed possession of the phone. Even the owners of her patients were dealt with by her receptionist, not her. That was all it was, unfamiliarity, she tried to convince herself, but it didn't stop the shiver that scurried up her spine. She forced herself to remember his question.

"Not at all, I just wanted to confirm that we had set our meeting as ten o'clock at Sugar Beach. I'd forgotten to write it down right away and worried I had messed it up in my recollection."

Tina congratulated herself on the reasonableness of the explanation. She was a busy working professional. It was entirely possible that she would have forgotten the appointment they'd set.

"That's what I was planning for. Is it still going to work for you and Tyler?"

"I expect so. I haven't told Tyler yet as I was afraid he'd be too excited to concentrate at school today." It was only a partial lie. It was true he'd probably be overexcited. But Tina hadn't told her son about the appointment for fear she had ruined it for him.

"That was probably reasonable," Clark said, sounding as though he approved of her parenting decision. It was ridiculous that Tina wanted to preen under the faint praise. But who ever offered her parenting praise, really? While it was true that she was often complimented on Tyler's behavior by his teachers, it was usually presented almost as though it were the teachers who had accomplished the task of raising him right. And all his teachers were women. That shouldn't matter, but Tina hadn't been praised by a man since she had been in college.

"Very well, then," Tina had answered, clearing her throat, and trying to sound like a normal human being. "We'll see you tomorrow, then."

"I'm looking forward to it."

Thankfully he had hung up right away and she hadn't been forced to come up with any other conversational gambits. She didn't know what to say to him that didn't involve grumbling on her part. She really needed to learn to communicate like an adult. Perhaps she would benefit from this arrangement almost as much as Tyler would, if it helped her learn to stop being such a grouch all the time. It felt as though this experience was showing her who she really was.

That brought her back to the present.

"Hey, bud, I have to tell you something."

Tyler wrinkled his forehead as he looked at her. Her tone must have alerted him to the fact that this wasn't just about what's for dinner.

"What's up, Mom?"

"My mind was a little bit scattered when you were telling me, did you get your homework all finished while you were at Grandma's?"

"That's not telling, Mom, that's asking," Tyler complained. "And yes, I got it all done. There wasn't much this weekend, which is great. Do we have anything planned for tomorrow? Or do we have chores we need to do?"

"We don't have much. If you're done your homework, we can get any chores done right after supper tonight and we'll be free for the whole weekend, as long as I don't have any emergencies. But we do have plans for tomorrow morning, as long as the weather cooperates."

"What is it?" Excitement was starting to mount in Tyler's voice as though he could guess what was going on. He was the smartest kid Tina knew, and she was exceedingly proud of him.

"You've been matched up with a guy named Clark, and we'll be meeting him at Sugar Beach tomorrow morning."

"All right!" Tyler cried out, pumping the air with his fists. Tina had to laugh. She wasn't even offended that her son was so excited about another adult entering his life. She was thrilled to be able to make him happy in this way. She only hoped it didn't come back to bite them in the bottom.

But not all adults disappointed you. She tried to remember that fact, repeating some of her favorite affirmations in her head as she endured the rest of the evening.

You are strong. You are capable. You are strong. You are capable. Those were her two favorites. The ones she believed the most. And she had them on repeat in her mind, helping her to cope.

Tyler couldn't get enough of hearing about Clark but unfortunately Tina didn't have much information to tell him.

She forced a laugh. "All I can really tell you, Ty, is that he doesn't have a criminal record, he didn't grow up around here, and he has two younger brothers. Oh, and he was also raised by a single mother, just like you. The rest we'll have to find out when we meet him tomorrow."

Tyler threw his arms around her waist and snuggled his face into her belly. "I love you, Mommy."

He never called her that anymore and her heart constricted at the endearment, knowing full well it was meant as such a gesture on his part.

"I love you too, bud," she said around the lump that was strangling her.

"Do you think he's going to like me?"

"I guarantee it," she answered immediately and sincerely. "Why wouldn't he?" she thought to ask. It wasn't like Tyler to express insecurities. She thought she had done a good job of hiding all her own from him. Tyler's shrug was uninformative.

"Like I told you, I don't know much about him, but I did meet him briefly at Aunt Rachel's wedding. He didn't strike me as being particularly stupid. And he would have to be not to like you."

"But what if he doesn't?" Tyler persisted.

Tina sat down so she could look her son in the eyes.

"I don't know what kind of things he's interested in, so maybe you won't have everything in common, but I would think for a man to sign up for a program like this, he's got to be pretty open to spending time doing boy-type stuff. And you're a normal kid with normal interests. I think you're the greatest thing to ever exist. While I might be a tad bit biased, I know I'm not completely off the mark. So, there is absolutely no reason why he wouldn't like you."

When Tyler didn't look completely convinced, Tina sighed and shook her head. "If you don't hit it off, I suppose we can call the school and ask for another match."

Tyler's eyes brightened. "You would do that?"

"Of course," Tina promised him. "But I really don't see any reason why we would have to go that route."

"I just like to have a back-up plan," Tyler said, making Tina grin.

"I'm afraid you get that from me."

Tyler returned her grin. "It's a good trait, I think. What are we going to take to the beach?" He changed the subject slightly, back to the matter of the next morning.

"Sunscreen, water, snacks, towels, blankets, a book for me, a frisbee for you," Tina rattled off. "I don't know, what else?"

"Do you think he might teach me how to throw a football?"

Tina laughed but fleetingly wondered why he had never learned such a thing at school or from one of his friends if it was something he wanted. "I didn't know you even wanted to know how to throw a football. Do we own one?"

Tyler nodded. "Remember, Jake gave me one. He was supposed to teach me how to throw it but then he was too busy with Aunt Rachel's wedding."

"Well, it was his wedding, too," Tina reminded him with a chuckle. "I'm sure Clark will be happy to toss around the football with you, just make sure we bring it." Before she had even finished saying the words Tyler had scampered away to find his ball and put it by the door.

"I'm not likely to forget it, but just in case," he explained to her as he came back to settle beside her on the sofa. "I hope he knows how to throw it."

"Is there a particular skill to it, then?"

Tyler laughed. "This is why I never bothered asking you to throw it with me. You have a hard enough time with a baseball."

"I do, but I've gotten better, haven't I?"

"You have, but so have I," Tyler said, proud of himself.

"And this is why I agreed for you to go into this program, I suppose. It takes some of the pressure off me to improve faster." Tina stared out the window to the darkening street beyond their house. "Ty, I need to talk to you about something serious, though, ok?"

Tyler's eyes widened, and he straightened up next to her, nodding.

"You know how I've always said you can't talk to strangers?"

Tyler nodded.

"I have never wanted to go into great detail with you about why not. But suffice it to say, not everyone has the best of intentions."

Tyler nodded again, but slower this time.

"I don't want to cast aspersions on this Clark fellow since his background check was clean and Jake and Rachel have known him for a few months, but you have to promise me, if you ever feel the least bit uncomfortable about him, you'll tell me. I promise I won't freak out, ok?"

Tyler stared at her for a moment but then nodded. "What are aspersions?" he asked, making her laugh.

"Well, I can't tell you exactly what an aspersion is, but casting aspersions means to slander someone. So, I wasn't trying to imply there is anything actually wrong with this man. We don't know him. But I don't want you to be so excited about the idea of him that you ignore any weird vibes you might get from him."

Tyler nodded slowly. "Ok, Mom," he said, thinking about it. "But I am already excited, so I'm not sure if I'll be able to watch for vibes. Do I even get vibes? Is that a mom thing?"

Tina smiled. "It might be a mom thing. I'll be watching closely, for sure, don't worry about that. I just wanted you to know that you can tell me even if you'd be disappointed."

Tyler nodded again, a little faster this time. "'K, no problem, Mom." He hopped up from the sofa. "I'd better get to bed, or I won't be able to get up in the morning."

"It's doubtful that's going to be the problem," Tina said on a laugh. "It's more likely that you will be too excited to fall asleep tonight."

"Maybe. What do you do to fall asleep when you're excited?"

Tina almost told him that she's never excited, but that would rain on his parade too much. And she supposed her various anxieties were a form of excitement, just not the type he was thinking of.

"I try to concentrate on my breathing, listen to it, slow it down, and think about my muscles that are tight from the excitement and try to get them to relax. I start at one end, like my head or my toes, and work my way up or down from there." When Tyler was looking at her as though he couldn't comprehend what she was saying she described it. "Like I lay in bed, close my eyes, and slow my breathing down. I might even count it out like, breathe in for five counts and out for five counts, you know? And then, with my eyes still closed, I think about my toes and think about them relaxing and going to sleep, then my ankles, then my calf muscles, then my knees, and so on. If I go slow enough and really think about them relaxing, I'm usually asleep before I get to my head."

Tyler looked skeptical, making Tina laugh. "Try it and see. Otherwise, you can just slowly count numbers or try to name all the state capitals. Something you know but might be boring. Just don't think about the thing that has you wound up. You should be asleep in no time flat."

Tyler hugged her and scampered off to the bathroom to brush his teeth, leaving his mother to her own stewing. Would she even be able to sleep that night? She'd have to use all her tricks not to think about the thing that had her worried. While she had given Tyler sound advice, it was going to be a challenge to follow it herself. This particular "excitement" might be just too big for her.

To her surprise, though, before long, it was morning and she had clearly slept quite soundly. She was finally starting to reap the benefits of eating better, she could see. The sugars in her previous diet must have been part of the problem, especially at night. At least it was one less thing she had to concern herself with that day, she thought as Tyler bounded into her room.

"It worked, Mom. I slept like a log. Did you?"

"I did, in fact, thanks for asking." She still felt tired, but that was a perpetual state for her, it would seem. Her doctor had suggested she might be low on certain nutrients, so she was trying to boost them with supplements, but it was a slow process. And her constant state of grumpy worry probably didn't help her much, either. "What do you think you'd like for breakfast? Should we have eggs and toast? Get some protein into you for all the running around you're likely to be doing?"

"Sure, sounds good. I'll do the toast, you do the eggs?" he asked as he left the room ahead of her.

"Deal. I'll meet you in the kitchen in ten minutes."

Tina reflected on what a great kid she had as she quickly went through her morning routine. She would do anything for him. Which was why she was going to meet this Clark fellow and watch her son get to know a stranger.

The face that looked back at her from the mirror was thinner than it had been even a week or two ago. That brought a smile to Tina's face. But she also noticed that it was as hard as ever. It was something about her eyes. She couldn't hide her constant animosity, at least not completely. It was pretty much only Tyler who never experienced the rough side of her tongue.

She ought to care and ought to try to curb her anger. But she couldn't find it within herself to care overmuch about how others perceived her. As long as Tyler was fine, everyone else could go fly a kite for all she cared.

But when it came to Tyler, she would do whatever needed to be done. And in this case, that meant she needed to be nice to Clark. But she didn't want him to think she was interested in him. So, what was she supposed to wear?

Tina frowned and then rolled her eyes at herself. She was ridiculous. They were going to the beach. It was far from a fashion parade. She quickly washed her face and slicked on the barest hint of makeup, just enough that she looked presentable, and put on the nearest clean but casual clothes she had. It was her behavior that would matter today, not her appearance, as long as she wasn't shameful in any way.

Tyler was waiting when she got to the kitchen. A glance at the clock told her she wasn't late. He was just that eager.

"Rushing isn't going to make him meet us any earlier than we arranged, Ty. I don't want you to make yourself sick from your excitement."

"Don't worry, Mom. I was just fast, is all. And I'm hungry, so hurry up."

Tina threw her hands in the air in mock surrender and made her way to the fridge to grab the eggs. Within minutes they were sitting in companionable silence, side by side at the breakfast bar.

"Did you sleep alright?" she asked around a mouthful of eggs, over medium, her favorite way to eat them.

"I dreamt about Dad," Tyler said, not exactly answering her question, but it told her most of what she needed to know.

"Was it a good one or a bad one?"

"Both, in a way," Tyler answered swinging his feet in a rare show of agitation. "We were playing catch, but then he disappeared."

It didn't take a psych degree to know what prompted that dream. "Is that what you're afraid is going to happen with Clark?"

Tyler shrugged and Tina sighed.

"I can't blame you for being nervous. And it's good to be wary. Don't give him your heart right off the bat because we really don't know this man at all. He isn't even from here, so I can see why you might think it's possible he'll disappear. But I'm sure you're going to have a great day today. That's what you need to focus on right now. Let the next day take care of itself for now."

Tyler nodded. "I know, Mom."

"But knowing it in your head is different than knowing it in your heart, isn't it?"

Tyler nodded again and then leaned over so that his head rested on her shoulder. Tina's heart constricted in her chest, and she almost had to cough to cover her reaction. But she didn't want anything to disturb the moment. She hated that it was her son's insecurity making him cling to her. But she loved that he still felt he *could* cling to her. It was an awful mixture.

"I wish Dad didn't die."

Tina swallowed to prevent her breakfast from returning.

"I know, bud," she answered so as not to lie.

"Do you miss him?"

How was she supposed to answer that impossible question?

"I miss the good times we used to have together, and I hate that he never got to know what a great kid you are."

"He loved baseball, right?"

116

"He did," Tina answered. "But don't feel you have to love it just because he did. You are your own person. You have to decide for yourself what you love, don't forget that."

"I won't," Tyler promised, even though Tina knew he hoped to emulate the father he'd never met. Tina only hoped she had told him good enough things but not too good, making it impossible for the boy to live up to what he imagined his father would have been.

Chapter Thirteen

His chiseled abs were the first or even the only thing she could see when they got out of the car.

Clark was waiting for them when they arrived, which took a weight off Tina's mind when that fact first registered there, but then it was swept out by the vision of the handsome contractor dressed for the beach.

Meeting at the beach was the worst possible idea.

He's not here to see you, you nitwit.

How could those possibly be real?

The conflicting but related thoughts chased each other through her mind until she realized Tyler was silent, so Tina pulled herself together. This wasn't about her and her personal issues with her own body. This was about Tyler and what he needed from life.

"You ready to have some fun, bud?" she asked her son as she climbed out of the car before stepping forward to shake Clark's hand in greeting like the professional she knew she was, not the insecure woman she was going to ignore that day. "Good morning, Clark, thank you for being on time."

Clark's grin made her grumpy, but she suppressed the impulse to scowl.

"This is late in the day for a contractor, so it wasn't hard to be on time. Plus, I was excited to be here," he answered her with only half his attention. "Hello, champ," he greeted Tyler. "You must be my new friend, Tyler. I've heard so many great things about you. I've been really looking forward to today."

To Tina's shock, Tyler only nodded and kicked the ground with his toe, not quite meeting Clark's gaze, even as he allowed the man to shake his hand in greeting.

Rather than being offended, though, Clark acted as though he hadn't even noticed, merely beginning to chat as though they had been friends for ages. Without asking for permission, he reached out and grabbed their things out of Tina's hands and walked toward the beach with purposeful strides, assuming they would follow him, which they did without much thought.

"I am so glad your mom suggested we meet at this beach. I'm new to the island, and I've never been to this one before. I'm used to going to the ones the tourists all go to. I don't know how you all have managed to keep the lid on this one. It's terrific. Have you been coming here all your life?"

"Yeah," Tyler answered, finally speaking, and appearing as though he were relaxing slightly. "Where do you normally go?"

"The beach I've been to most is the one close to the ferry dock," Clark said.

"Oh no, that one's the worst," Tyler exclaimed. "It's a good thing my mom told you, then, for sure."

"It sure is." Clark agreed with a grin that seemed to include Tina, but she kept her expression neutral lest she allow her hormones out of the box she'd tucked them into ten years before. Clark turned his focus back to Tyler. "You brought a football, that's terrific. I haven't had a chance to throw one around in a few months."

"Does that mean you can teach me how to throw it, then?" Tyler asked, eagerness vibrating through him and overriding his previous anxiety about making this new acquaintance.

"Sure, I can," Clark agreed immediately. "Let's just get your mom situated and then we can throw until our shoulders give out."

Tyler laughed as though the man had told the funniest joke on earth but later, while Tina was watching them throw the ball over and over, she suspected that it was possible they would have very sore shoulders later.

As she sat watching them surreptitiously over the edge of the book she wanted to read but couldn't concentrate on, Tina thought about how helpful Clark had been as he helped her spread the blanket between the dunes and the edge of the surf, making sure she was settled comfortably before he went off with Tyler. It had made her feel cared for in a way that she hadn't experienced in years. It also made her highly uncomfortable. She was decidedly unused to being cared for by anyone. It made her suspicious of the man's motives. There was no need to toady to her. It made her nervous and made her question everything about him. It also made her feel ridiculous.

Tina sighed. She *was* ridiculous. But one could never be too careful when it came to your child's safety.

Well, maybe you could.

According to Angela, if you were too overprotective you put the child at risk of never learning to judge things for themselves or always being terrified of everything. She didn't want either of those outcomes for Tyler. Tina thought she had done a pretty good job up until now of curbing her urge to wrap him in bubble wrap, but this particular scenario had her spun all out of control.

It was probably exacerbated by the fact that she had her own mixed-up feelings about this man in particular, on top of her convoluted feelings about men in general.

Not every man was going to be like Karl.

She had to remember that. And maybe even Karl wouldn't have been like Karl eventually. They were very young when he died. He might have grown out of his narcissistic tendencies. Not that narcissists change, according to Angela. But perhaps he wasn't a true narcissist. It had just seemed that way because he was a self-absorbed young man. He might have outgrown that. There was no way he could have looked at Tyler and not fallen in love with him immediately.

It had been different for Tina because Tyler was actually inside her. He was literally a part of her. Of course, genetically he was also a part of Karl. But it would be different for a man, not having had that actual literal physical connection. Forty weeks is a long time to be connected to something. Or someone.

So, she tried to still her impulsive reactions and settled back to watch.

Tyler was having a blast. Clark appeared to be enjoying himself immensely as well. Tina was far from bored, despite the tumult rioting through her or it might be more accurate to say that because of the tumult she couldn't possibly be bored. But there was also nothing boring about watching her beloved son have a good time. There was also nothing boring about the very good-looking man who was playing with her son.

This is how Tyler's life should have been.

The thought came from her subconscious and nearly choked her with regret over how her and Tyler's lives had turned out, but she immediately rejected the thought.

While it was true that no one wished their child to have only one parent, she and Tyler had done the best that they could and according to everyone, not just her own biased opinion, Tyler was a fantastic little man. He hadn't turned out so bad despite the lemon he had been dealt in the father department. And now, here was a decent guy willing to help him learn the few things Tina couldn't contribute to his education.

Like how to throw a spiral.

Tina did not for a second think a girl couldn't throw a perfectly good spiral. Just that she, Doctor Tina, couldn't throw a spiral if her life had depended on it. And so here they were. And even her untrained eye could see that Tyler was doing great.

He was a fast study about everything. It was a blessing for him in most ways. But it would be a challenge for him to be, well, challenged as he grew older. Tina believed, and she was supported by her psychology-loving best friend Angela on this, that kids thrived and grew on being challenged. If Tyler was too smart, that was going to make it difficult for him.

Tina shook her head. She was certainly on a worry roll today. Worrying that her son was too smart was taking it a touch too far, even for her. Helping him be successful even if he was very smart was going to be one of the easier challenges. And for now, he was definitely exercising a different form of intelligence than usual. And having a blast while doing it.

She couldn't help but be proud of his ability and agility even though he had obviously not gotten that from her. Tina refused to look down at her own bulges that attested to her lack of athleticism. That was not something she was going to give thought to today. She had enough acid nibbling at the edges of her digestive tract without adding that to the mix, she assured herself.

Forcing her eyes back to the book in her hands, she tried to get her brain to focus but even without watching them, Tina was highly aware of what Clark and Tyler were doing. Her reactions to watching the man participating in the same sport as her son were very different, that was for sure.

She almost couldn't identify the sensations; it had been so long since she had experienced them. But she was fairly sure it was attraction, which appalled her. She had no interest in being attracted to anyone, let alone the guy who would be spending time with her son.

Why did she like to complicate her life at every turn?

Not that she was enjoying this. Well, to be honest, it was kind of nice to feel attraction again. But it was ill-timed, inappropriate, and inconvenient. She could probably think of more adjectives to add to the list, but those were plenty. She had thought that part of her had died the first time her young husband had raised his hand toward her or called her an ugly name. Perhaps it had just been dormant.

Well, it could stay dormant a little longer, Tina thought with a grumble. She had no time for such nonsense. Not until Tyler was fully grown.

She was just beginning to feel secure. The final payment on her and Karl's student loans had just cleared her bank account two weeks ago, not leaving it completely empty.

That was when she knew they were going to be okay. Not that she had really been so fearful before that. Not for at least a few years, anyway. The worst of the terror had been when she had gone into labor a couple weeks early, while she was still trying to finish her internship. She had worried it would derail finishing her degree. But the school had been very understanding, and the veterinarian she had been interning for had written her such a glowing recommendation that her college had considered it finished. It had been the only time in her adult life she had been given a break. And it was the thing that had saved her and Tyler's future.

Of course, there had been her next internship, in New York City, but that had at least been a paid position. Not very much pay, but enough that she had been able to pay their rent and keep them fed.

And then they'd finally moved to the Cape, and she'd set up her clinic and here they were. Tyler was ten years old, her student debts were finally paid off, they had a small little house that she at least owned a portion of. Now that her student debt was paid off, she should be able to increase her payments on the house a little bit. She knew they would penalize her if she paid it off too aggressively, but she was pretty sure she'd be able to pay some extra.

Life was starting to appear doable for the first time in her adult life.

She was going to have to figure out what to do with her life now that she didn't feel as though she were merely surviving.

Of course, she had already started on the first step – getting her health in order. She finally did glance down at her bulges, but just to reaffirm for herself that they were indeed shrinking. Not by a lot, but at least some. That was progress. As long as there was progress, she could carry on. It was stagnation that made her mental.

Just thinking about it made her anxiety start to climb, so she turned her focus toward the waves. There was nothing more reassuring than waves, in Tina's opinion. They never stopped coming to shore. Even when the tide was going down, the waves kept coming to shore. You could almost line up your breathing with the waves, at times, but not always, so she wouldn't attempt it today. She needed to get her breathing and heart rate under control, or she'd pass out and cause a stir that would ruin Tyler's day.

She almost laughed. Passing out would surely ruin her day, too.

Tina tried to think of the affirmations she wanted to tell herself that day. She couldn't decide if she actually believed in that woo-woo stuff, but she did know that if you told yourself too much negativity, if you believed that negativity, it became true. So, the opposite was likely to do the same thing. And she would much rather talk herself into something positive than something negative.

I am healthy. I am wealthy. I am pretty. She snorted softly over that one, which pulled her out of the mindset she was trying to create. All right. She might not be that pretty, but she did believe that pretty was a state of mind. She was keeping that one.

I am healthy. I am wealthy. I am pretty. I am kind.

Okay. That last one might be a stretch, too. But she wanted to be kind. So, she would continue to fake it until she could make it a reality. Look at her. She hadn't ruined this excursion for Tyler. Of course, that could be more a testament to Clark's being raised by a fine woman than to anything she had or had not done.

That thought made her think back to the conversation she had had with Clark's mother the day he'd given her the phone number. The woman had been delightful. And so hopeful that her son was pursuing a courtship.

Courtship. What a quaint, old-fashioned word. Tina might like to be courted someday. But who would want a fat, cranky old lady like her?

I am healthy. I am wealthy. I am pretty. I am kind.

She got through the affirmations without snorting her derision this time, so that was progress. Perhaps she could be more like Clark's mom one day. She might need to talk to the woman again.

"Are you quite certain he isn't going to try courting you at the same time?"

Tina had laughed in surprise. She had just explained to Mrs. Clark that her son had been matched with Tina's son in a program at Tyler's school.

"I had hoped he would decide to make children of his own, but I suppose this is more expedient," the older woman had sighed.

"Well, he's far from being too old, ma'am. Perhaps he'll still go that route later."

"Maybe you could help him see the benefits of marriage and babies."

It had been necessary for Tina to literally bite her tongue to prevent the caustic words from leaving her mouth that had been her first reaction. Instead, she had just murmured something nonsensical and extricated herself from the conversation.

It didn't prove anything. As she had told Clark, even serial killers had mothers. But from every movie and tv show she'd ever seen, the mothers of serial killers were usually psycho pieces of work themselves. Clark's mother had been the sweetest woman Tina had talked to in ages. She had asked all about Tyler and and even told Tina a few things about Clark at Tyler's age. It had been endearing. But Tina didn't want to feel endearment for Clark, she reminded herself.

Clark had been exactly the same age as Tyler was now when his father had walked out on their family. Tina wondered what Angela would say about that. Probably some psychobabble about Clark overcompensating for his childhood. But Tina suspected he was trying to make sure some other kid didn't have the feelings he had experienced at that age.

Of course, it was different for Tyler. He didn't know his father had walked out on him. He only knew his father was dead. Tina hoped that made it better. That was why she had never told anyone the full story. She couldn't bear for Tyler to know. It was much more acceptable for him to be angry at the inevitableness of death rather than to know that his father hadn't wanted him to exist. Surely that would have been worse for his psyche than just not having a father in his life.

But from what she could see, Clark had turned out pretty good. Or he was better at hiding his issues than most were. Of course, they hadn't yet done anything to make him angry. That thought clutched in Tina's mind and made her stomach roll over. Not that she wanted to encourage Tyler to make the man angry, but Tina wondered if maybe they should do so, just to see how he would react. She couldn't entrust him with her son if there was any fear that he might lash out.

Not that Tyler would ever do anything to make anyone angry. But Tina hadn't thought the things she did that made Karl angry were any big deal. Sometimes you just couldn't know what someone's triggers were.

Of course, that same reasoning meant there was no way she could know how to set Clark off in order to see how he would react.

Tina sighed.

She really ought to get professional counselling. There was only so much self-help books could do, she supposed. Of course, it was likely that she was a little more messed up than the average person. She had lived an idyllic childhood, in her estimation, even if her parents were less attentive than those of some of her friends. But she had both a mom and a dad and they were still married to one another and still even seemed to get along reasonably well. They were generous with their time to help her out with Tyler, especially when he had been pre-school age. That couldn't have been what they expected to do with their lives.

Not that Tina had ever heard them discuss fun retirement plans.

Another sigh escaped her. She supposed, now that she had gotten out from under that massive debt, she ought to start thinking about retirement. She rolled her eyes. Retirement was a long way off a she was still on the sunny side of thirty-five. But she knew many started thinking on retirement plans as soon as they started their first job. Tina hadn't had that particular luxury.

She hadn't had any luxuries, to be honest. But now they could start having a few, she supposed. They would have to start thinking of treats as something other than food. Perhaps a manicure from time to time. The problem with that is that it would be only for her, not Tyler, unlike food treats where their tastes were nearly the same.

She would have to discuss it with Tyler. He was old enough to have input on this sort of thing now.

This is where a partner would come in handy, she realized and her gaze strayed toward Clark once more, for which she quickly reprimanded herself.

Just because he was handsome and single did not mean he was partner potential!

She was the worst. Vacillating between thinking he was possibly a psycho and questioning his desire to befriend her kid to thinking he was husband potential in the space of a few hours was a bit extreme even for her. Tina shifted her gaze back to the rolling surf. Perhaps she should go and dunk herself in. That would certainly cool her thoughts.

But the Atlantic was a cold body of water, and she wasn't hot enough to warrant such a treatment quite yet. Perhaps just a walk would do to turn her thoughts to something more productive. She suited her thoughts to actions and set out at a brisk walk.

"Tina, hey, how's it going?"

The sound of a surprised but delighted female voice coming from behind her had Tina turning to see who was calling her.

"Evelyn, what a surprise," she returned with a grin, slowing her pace so the other woman could catch up.

"Any development in your situation?" Evelyn asked, sounding cryptic and making Tina laugh out loud.

"A major development," she said and gestured over her shoulder where Tyler could be heard crowing with delight over his most recent throw or catch or whatever they were doing at the moment. "Tyler might not be able to use his arm for a week after this, but he's having the time of his life at the moment, so I don't have the heart to warn him any further than Clark already did."

"Oh good, so you didn't run him off as you had feared," Evelyn replied with a light laugh. "And are you coping alright with the situation?"

"Not particularly. Well, maybe," Tina answered and shook her head.

Chapter Fourteen

Rather than making her angry, Evelyn's laughter actually caused joy to rise up within Tina. Or she supposed that was what the sensation would be called. She didn't feel it terribly often and when she did, it was usually in connection with Tyler or something he had done or accomplished. Not something she had done. But making someone laugh with genuine amusement felt like an accomplishment of her own, and her chest welled with pride following the joy.

Perhaps she wasn't the worst wretch on the island after all. That was a pleasant thought to consider. And she was coping. She had managed not to Google Clark nor contact any of his social media friends. And she had only given his social media accounts a cursory search. Would he really post about any criminal activities anyway? If he was that stupid the background check would have picked it up.

Tina rolled her eyes again. Clearly her progress was in baby step increments.

"What are you doing here on a Saturday? From what I understand, you usually stick close to home on the weekends," Tina remarked. "Is everything okay?"

Evelyn shrugged and her light laugh sounded forced or fake somehow. Tina searched her face. She really needed to get better at not be excessively absorbed in her own issues.

"Yeah, it's fine. Just my husband had to go away for work again, and I wanted a change of scenery, so I wasn't reminded of how empty my house is."

"Do you want to hang out with us? It might make it less weird that I'm watching my son play with a grown man." But then Tina remembered her friend's other issue. "Or will that make it even harder for you?"

"Well, if you need me, I'll be glad to come," Evelyn said generously, but Tina could hear the hint of reluctance in her tone.

"No, no, I'm really fine. I'm trying to read that book you and Rachel recommended. I should get back to it. I just needed to burn off a little of my own thoughts in order to concentrate on it."

"Oh, the one Rachel's mentor just released?" Evelyn asked with a genuine smile.

"That's the one. The blurb on the back makes it sound fascinating, but I haven't been gripped by it yet."

Evelyn glanced back toward Clark and Tyler. "That's not likely the book's fault," she commented in a dry tone, making Tina laugh.

"Yeah, probably not." Tina turned the subject again. "Do you think we'll ever see Rachel's book in print?" she asked, referring to their friend's dreams of becoming an historical fiction author.

"Have you read any of her work? She's really good. I would have thought she'd be in every bookstore by now. But from what I understand, these things take much longer than you'd realize."

"Hmmm." Tina made a noncommittal sound, not sure what to say and her thoughts were straying once more. She needed a more rigorous hike before returning to her blanket and her surveying of her son and his new friend.

Evelyn must have had a similar thought. "I need to blow off a little steam, Tina. It was nice to bump into you, but I'm going to head the other way. Text me if you need me to come and save you from homicidal thoughts," she added with a light laugh. "Otherwise, I'll see you soon."

Tina returned the other woman's smile and wave and then set off briskly herself. It had been pleasant to run into Evelyn. It was one more reminder that Tina needed to count her own blessings. Her circumstances, while not perfectly ideal, were better than some others.

It seemed to Tina that everyone was struggling with something. She was far from the only one. On the surface, Evelyn's life appeared idyllic. But the poor woman wanted children and so far, she hadn't been able to have any. There were so many unfortunate souls in the world, Tina wondered why Evelyn and her husband didn't just foster or adopt, but that was such a highly personal matter, she had never dared to ask the question. Even her acerbic tongue had limits. That was good to know, she thought with a wry twist of her lips as she set off at a brisk pace, hoping to leave her twisted thoughts behind.

A half hour later, Tina was feeling a little more settled into her soul when she returned to her spot on the beach. That settled feeling didn't last long. She couldn't see Tyler.

Fear gripped her hard. Followed swiftly by anger. Anger at herself mostly for being so foolish as to let down her guard. But anger at Clark, the school, the entire world was eating at the edges of her reason.

Pulling out her phone to place a call to the emergency services, Tina was just about to press the button when she heard Tyler's voice.

"Mom, hey Mom, there you are!"

There were not enough breathing exercises in the world that could calm her down enough for this situation.

"Where have you been? I almost called 9-1-1!" She yelled the words in a shrill voice Tyler certainly didn't recognize.

Of course, he didn't recognize the voice, she had never used it before. She felt bile rising in her throat and almost vomited right there. Only fury and determination prevented it.

"You weren't here," Tyler pointed out. "I had to pee. And despite the fact that everyone I know does it, you always said it's too gross for words to pee in the ocean, so we had to go find the washroom."

"And there was no cell service to tell me where you had gone?"

Her fury was no longer narrowing her vision, but it was still very evident in her voice.

Tyler only stared at her, not understanding the situation, but Clark quickly spoke up. "That's my fault, Doctor Tina. We thought we'd just be a second. We actually were just a second, or probably little more than a minute, so we figured, since we couldn't see you in either direction, we thought we'd be back before you."

"That isn't a good enough explanation. We agreed for you to be here. Nowhere else. Taking my son somewhere else required my permission. At the barest minimum a heads up. A text message or a phone call was most definitely called for. I think our day is done here. Gather your things, Tyler, we have to go."

Tina's stomach heaved again as she noted the disappointment etching itself on her son's face. He couldn't possibly understand all the risks that had been taken that day. But none of it was his fault. She should never have agreed to this arrangement. She should never have gone for a walk. She was the idiot. But she had told them she was going. They hadn't told her what they were doing. That wasn't Tyler's fault. The adult in the situation was the one at fault.

"Doctor Tina, listen, I'm so sorry."

"That's fine, Clark. But I cannot entrust my son to someone who cannot be responsible for such a little thing. If you can't look after the little things, you can't be trusted with the big things. How much trouble would it be to send a text message?"

She had truly tried to restrain her mouth, but she was shouting by the time she got to the end of her question and finally bit down on the inside of her cheek to stem the words. She might be being slightly unreasonable. They had only gone to the washroom. But she had been extremely clear about her reservations about the entire arrangement. The man was irresponsible and not to be trusted with her son. She would find some other way for Tyler to get involved in the activities he was interested in. Having one other adult become an important figure in his life was too big a risk. And that had been well and proven that day.

"Come on, Tyler, time to go. Say your goodbyes to Clark."

"Can we come back next week?" Tyler asked, a quaver clear in his voice. Tina had to harden her heart in order to resist.

"I'll talk to you about it in the car, Tyler."

Tyler stared at her, an unfamiliar expression of mutiny crossing his features.

"But I need to know if this is goodbye or see you later," he insisted.

"I told you to say goodbye, Tyler."

Both male faces staring at her had nearly identical expressions of disbelief before Clark blinked and turned to Tyler.

"You've got to listen to your mother, buddy. I had a blast with you today. I hope I can see you again but if not, just know that it was completely my fault, not yours. And keep practicing that throw, you've got a good one. You might need to put a little ice on that shoulder tonight, though."

The way Tyler's chin was quivering made Tina have to glance away and reassure herself that she was doing the right thing. Her son was her priority. He was too young to understand the risks that strangers could pose. Especially large, male strangers.

Even large, males you knew well could harm you irrevocably. Tina couldn't allow that to happen to her beloved boy.

But was she the one causing the harm this time?

That thought was circling her mind uncontrollably as they drove away to the sound of Tyler's nearly silent efforts not to cry. Tina's heart broke into about three million pieces at each of his huffing and shuddering little breaths.

"Tyler, bud, you have to understand."

"No, Mom, I don't have to. Clark wasn't going to hurt me in any way. He wouldn't even let me go into the bathroom by myself, just like you. Except with him, I was able to go into the men's room like I'm supposed to. He told me to go into a stall so no one could watch me, which was a bit weird, but he stayed outside my door like he was guarding it. He even watched while I washed my hands. It would have been completely

135

embarrassing except no one else was in there. He didn't touch me. He didn't say anything weird to me. He just didn't text you. That we were going to the bathroom. A completely and totally normal thing that people have to do when they try to stay hydrated like their mother told them to do."

It wasn't exactly disrespectful, but it was getting awfully close. However Tina couldn't really fault what her son was saying. He was using his words, in a much better way than she had done, if Tina was being honest with herself.

"I don't even know what you're so afraid of him doing to me. Do you think he's going to beat me up? Or steal me? I don't think kidnappings are nearly as common as they were in the 90s, Mom." Tyler wasn't being sarcastic. He knew that was a fear she had been raised on. She had always tried not to put her fears onto her son. And she had obviously succeeded in that regard if he knew about the kidnappings and yet didn't fear them himself like she always had at his age.

"There are worse things than being kidnapped or beaten up, Tyler. Unspeakable things. But you're right, Clark doesn't give me those vibes at all. Thank you for telling me that he sent you into a stall. Were you disappointed not to use a urinal your first time into a men's room?"

"It wasn't my first time. Grandpa sometimes takes me. But no, I was glad not to use the urinal for the first time in front of Clark."

Tina's stomach clenched again but she tried to stay calm as she asked him, "Why not?"

"What if I missed? Or wasn't tall enough? How embarrassing would that have been?"

Tina actually laughed. She didn't think she would ever be able to laugh again, but she did and was relieved when Tyler joined her in laughing.

"If I swear to you that it will never happen again, that we'll never forget to text you for any reason, and if I do all the yard work and house chores for two weeks, could you please let me see Clark again? If he even wants to after this. He might think I'm too much trouble to bother with."

Tina's stomach heaved once more, and she almost had to pull over to empty the contents of her stomach at her son's words. There was no accusation in them. He wasn't even angry with her. Just disappointed all the way down to the tips of his toes. He accepted that his mother was irrational, and he loved her anyway. But he clearly hoped, just this once, if he bargained hard enough, she would see her way clear to being a little less irrational than usual. Tina wasn't sure where he got his sanity. It obviously wasn't from either of his parents. Had she accidentally switched him at birth?

Tina's heart constricted. That was the craziest thing she had thought in her life. Tyler was her son even if he was saner than her. Even his cowlicks matched hers.

"I'll think about it, Tyler," was all she could promise at that point. Maybe if her heart recovered from its attack of fear that afternoon, she would be able to give it calm and sober consideration. To his credit, Tyler didn't even pout. But somehow that made Tina feel even worse. He was right. Probably the things she feared most wouldn't happen. But the slightest chance was just too much for this mama's heart to bear. But would her protection of him also do harm?

Chapter Fifteen

What just happened?

Clark watched as the car's taillights disappeared down the road and tried to work it out in his head. Was the woman a total nut case? Or was she a normal mother who was protecting her kid? The friend who had introduced him to the program at the school had seemed to indicate that the single parents who were sending their kids into the program were thrilled to have them off their hands for a while.

Not so with Doctor Tina, that was for sure.

She was a beautiful woman but clearly neurotic. It was such a shame. He had been having such a fun afternoon with Tyler. Clark would have loved to establish a buddy relationship with the kid.

Clark's heart panged. He wished he had a kid of his own just like Tyler. It was such a shame he hadn't started having kids at a younger age like the good doctor had done.

Of course, that didn't seem to have worked out in her psychological favor, though, Clark thought with a twist of his lips.

What was he going to do about it?

Should he contact the school and get matched with another kid? Not to say that they were interchangeable. He had quite liked Tyler and the kid seemed to take to him, too. That wasn't guaranteed to happen with another boy. And with a mother like his, Tyler could really use a normal adult in his life.

Would he be able to convince the crazy veterinarian that she should take another chance on him? What a stupid mistake for him to have made. It had probably been a test and he failed it. He should have seen it coming. He should have been better than that. In his old corporate days, he would have seen such a test coming. But he had relaxed since he'd settled on this island, and that had failed him today.

Considering how skittish she had been from the beginning, he should have been extra careful about messaging her about any slight deviation. But he hadn't considered taking the kid for a wizz was a deviation of anything she had planned.

But since she had evidenced such distrust of him, he should have realized her not seeing them immediately would have triggered whatever fears she had. He was the bonehead. And he needed to apologize again, most sincerely.

But how do you say sorry to a woman who thought you were going to steal or harm her kid? What sends that sort of message? Would flowers just be weird? Or would she love them? Would a florist be able to advise him? Which shade of flower says please trust me, I'm not a stalker?

Clark's ready humor came to his rescue, and he was able to finally find a laugh within his soul. But he still felt terrible about the way the morning had ended. And he hadn't even had any snacks, so now he was both grumpy and hungry.

With a sigh, Clark hopped into his truck and set out to find some lunch and plan out exactly what he could say to the woman to convince her to give him one more chance.

Unfortunately, the day got away from him before he had figured out any viable solution, and so he was nervous and almost dismayed when his phone rang and he saw Doctor Tina flash on his screen.

"Hello?" He answered it as a question even though he knew who was calling. Clark hated to feel wrong-footed, but that was exactly his state of mind in that moment.

"Clark, it's Tina, Tyler's mom," she started before clearing her throat, giving away her own nerves at the conversation. Contrarily, knowing she was nervous put Clark more at ease.

"Good evening, Tina, thank you for calling. I wasn't sure if I should call you or not, but I wanted to tell you again how sorry I was or am that we stepped away for a moment without telling you."

"You shouldn't have done that, but it was an honest mistake, and I shouldn't have freaked out on you for it. So, I'm sorry, too." Clark could hear her take a deep breath as though to steel her nerves for what she was about to say next. Clark held his breath, too, unsure what she might be about to say. He actually heard her swallow and even though she was the crankiest person he had ever met, his heart went out to her. She was obviously a deeply caring and protective mother. He couldn't fault any woman for that.

"Tyler really had a good time with you today. I should have listened to your explanation and listened to what Tyler had to say before making a decision and cutting the day short."

She paused again, blowing out a breath of either nervous or angry air. Clark couldn't quite tell. And since Tina seemed to always be angry, he suspected it might be more that than nerves. His own nerves crept back. *What was she going to say?* Thankfully he didn't have to wait too long. She continued.

"If my overprotective response hasn't put you off spending time with Tyler, he would really appreciate another chance to throw a ball with you."

Clark was impressed despite himself. He never would have thought she would ask for a do-over. But it was clearly evident she loved her son, and it was only because of that, she was trying to overcome her fears. She wasn't wrong to be protective. He couldn't blame her for that. There were monsters in the world. And he couldn't say what she might have experienced in her life. It was further testament to her love for her son that she was trying to get around those fears. For that reason alone, never mind all the other reasons, he should have been all the more careful.

"I would really like that. When might be good for you two? I know he has school, so is a midweek afternoon or evening out of the question? Or tomorrow afternoon?"

Tina laughed lightly even though it sounded a little forced to Clark's ears. "He was trying to demonstrate how responsible he is so I would trust him to spend time with you. So, there isn't a single chore left to be done in this house. If you are available tomorrow, he actually is, too. But I know you weren't expecting to see us tomorrow, so he will understand if that's too short notice."

Clark relaxed and shook his head even though she couldn't see him.

"Actually, I had thought we'd be tied up all day today, so I took advantage of the sudden free time to get my stuff done, too. So, I'm completely open tomorrow. What sorts of things do you two enjoy doing?"

"Well, considering that I behaved badly, my preferences don't need to come into the discussion at all. But one of Tyler's favorite things is to grab hotdogs by the pier and watch the fishermen. If you could teach him how to fish or especially if you know how to skip rocks, either of those would be a delight for him."

"Fishing isn't my very favorite activity, although I would be willing to do it with him. I'm not sure if I even have a rod anymore. So, let's save that for another day. I'd love to show him how to skip rocks. But his shoulder might be too sore tomorrow after all the throwing today." He paused in thought for a moment. "How does he feel about soccer?"

When Tina laughed this time, it sounded a little more genuine. "I'm not sure if he has feelings about soccer aside from if it's a sport, he'd love to learn about it."

"Good, I'll bring my soccer ball, too. If we aren't up for the stones, we can kick around the ball and run some drills or something."

Tina's laughter, even lighter this time, lightened Clark's mood all the more. "You sound like a coach all of a sudden," she said.

"I guess that's what I'm hoping to be, in a way," he agreed with a grin she obviously couldn't see over the phone, but it lightened his spirit anyway. "If you both will let me."

"Thanks for trying to understand about my concerns, Clark. And for not holding them against Tyler. He's the best kid and he really wants this. I would hate to prevent him from having some great experiences."

Clark relaxed back into the armchair he was sitting on. He had been on its edge, nervous when he'd seen who was calling him. But now that the conversation was turning out much better than he'd expected, he was able to take his usual, casual pose.

"So, what's Tyler into? What sorts of things do you think he'd enjoy doing with me?"

Tina's laugh seemed truly genuine this time even if it sounded a little rusty. He tried to give her the benefit of the doubt. She was obviously a very caring mother even if she seemed like a crank to everyone else. From what Clark had been able to see of her son, he was a bright, personable kid. That didn't happen just through genetics or by accident. Clearly his mother had done things well. So, she evidently saved the caustic side of herself for everyone else.

"I want to say he's into everything but that likely wouldn't be terribly helpful to you if you're trying to think of things to plan together." She paused for a moment, perhaps to gather her thoughts. "Part of the reason that I finally agreed for him to try this program is because I realized he probably might be into things that I have no idea about. I am only one person and I only have so many ideas or so much ability, you know? Like I was never a boy, obviously. So, I have zero interest in bugs or cars or sports. Not to say that girls can't be interested in those things, of course, but I certainly wasn't. And I think he might be. Definitely the sports. I tried, especially when he was little. But as you could see today, he has definitely outgrown my abilities or skills."

Clark nodded again even though she couldn't see him through the phone. She kept talking, as though she couldn't stem the tide of words about her favorite subject.

"There are all sorts of things he'd probably be interested in. Like exploring the woods or nature more than I've been able to do with him. He and I have done some hiking in some of the national forests. But he'd probably love to do cave exploration or rock climbing or camping. Things that are a little more extreme than what I've been capable of doing." She paused briefly but then quickly added, "Of course, if you aren't into those things, I'm pretty sure he'd like to try anything you suggest. He's just thrilled to have another adult that isn't his mom or grandparents."

"Why do you suppose that is?" Clark asked.

"He longs for a father," Tina said softly but then quickly added. "Not to say he's looking to you to be his dad, no pressure, right?" she said with a nervous laugh. "But that sort of male influence. Someone other than his mom. I've tried to do my best, but I think kids thrive with the attentions of two parents as a counterbalance. My parents have helped us immensely, but my dad isn't energetic. He'd happily do puzzles with Tyler all day long, but he isn't going to go for a bike ride with him. I have some cousins who live in other states who stay in touch with my parents but aren't terribly interested in me and Tyler. They visit sometimes but don't take time to spend with him. He has friends from school, but I haven't been the best about being friendly with their parents, no surprise, right? So, his friends' dads haven't taken a great deal of interest in him either."

She laughed again, as though embarrassed, perhaps not meaning to reveal so much.

"Families are weird, aren't they?" she finally asked, as though at a conclusion of her explanation.

"They definitely are. I'll tell you about mine some time and you'll see yours is quite average."

"That will be good to know," she finally said, sounding softer than he'd ever heard her, as though the rollercoaster of the day had worn her out.

Clark wanted to be angry with her or dislike her, but he just couldn't for some strange reason. He didn't think it was just because she was so good looking. Surely, he wasn't so shallow. Yes, she could tighten up in a couple of places but really, who couldn't? She was nearly perfect in all respects from a physical perspective. And then she would open her mouth and one's perspective would be changed.

It was unfortunate for the poor woman, really. And for Tyler, when one thought about it. If his mother wasn't so grouchy, perhaps she could have remarried and provided the father figure the boy so clearly wanted.

But as their conversation carried on talking about various interests they held in common and how Tyler was doing in school, he was almost able to forget the awkward morning they'd had and the furious, biting words she often used.

She certainly wasn't using them now.

She wasn't flirting with him, though, that was certain, which was often the interactions he had with women he encountered. They were just having a normal, interesting conversation. Despite how busy she evidently was, she was still well-read and conversant on a wide range of subjects. Some of it likely stemmed from her university days, but she had obviously not left learning entirely.

She also seemed very surprised that he was so well-read.

Her inner shrew was showing again in little things. Like that very surprise about how their opinions lined up. Clark wanted to laugh but wasn't sure if it would

145

end their conversation. Despite her grouchy tendencies, he actually enjoyed her dry wit when it showed through.

But it was clearly evident that she thought he was an uneducated neanderthal. Most likely because he worked in construction. He wondered if she thought the same of Jake.

"So how do you know Jake and Rachel?" he asked in a lull in the conversation.

"I went to school with them. High School, anyway. Rachel only moved to the island when she was around thirteen, I think."

"Were you friends with them back then?"

"Sort of. Yes, with Rachel, especially at times. Kids can be beasts. Girls in particular, I think. So, we weren't always friends. But we did track and field together."

Clark tried to control his surprise over that. Maybe she wasn't the only one with stereotypical ideas about the other. Looking at her, you wouldn't guess track star right off the bat. But the freshman fifteen plus having a child could do all sorts of unwelcome things to a body, he supposed. He managed to keep himself from expressing his surprise and was glad the conversation wasn't taking place in person, as it would likely be written on his face.

"What sports were you into in school?" She either didn't notice his hesitation or she was avoiding addressing it, just carrying on the conversation.

"Football," he answered, "among others. But that was my main sport. I went to uni on a scholarship."

"A football scholarship?" she asked for clarification.

"Yeah," he replied, wishing he could see her face when she took that in.

"Which spot did you play?" she asked and then laughed. "That's likely the wrong word. But were you the one running with the ball or were you one of the goons trying to keep the others away?"

Clark laughed. "I played multiple positions in my time at school," not wanting to brag, he didn't tell her that he had been the quarterback and had NFL teams trying to recruit him, not that she would understand what that meant. It had been a great way to get his education, but it wasn't something he wanted to pursue after that.

"Did you ever have any horrific injuries? I've heard terrible things about some football injuries."

"I was one of the lucky ones. To my knowledge, I never got a concussion. Some breaks, strains, and sprains, of course, but not the worst of the injuries."

He could almost hear her nod. "That's good. I guess that's why you were so good at teaching Tyler how to throw. But I would really prefer him not to get too interested in football. The brain is such a sensitive organ, you know?"

"Yeah, I know."

"So, were you too busy with your team to focus on studies?" she asked, fueling his feeling of insult.

"I was not, as a matter of fact. The school I went to was pretty good about not placing football over academics, unlike some of the schools I could have gone to. You had to maintain a certain average in order to stay on the team, just like in high school."

Chapter Sixteen

Heat filled Tina's chest. She had likely insulted Clark once more. She hadn't meant to, of course. Most people probably didn't insult others intentionally unless they were psychotic. Of course, Clark could probably be excused for thinking she was psycho.

Tina took a deep breath, intending to apologize but then wondered if that would open a whole other kettle of fish. Her mind raced. *What would Evelyn do? What would Angela do?* Well, they wouldn't be in this particular situation, she realized with a roll of her eyes.

"So, what did you study, then?" she finally asked, hoping she hadn't left too awkward a pause.

"Business management." His clipped tone told her he was at least slightly irritated with her and her questions.

"Business management is rather vague," Tina remarked mildly. "Did you enjoy your studies?"

"I did, actually. Far more than the actual work ended up being, though."

"Oh dear, that's unfortunate. What didn't you like about it?"

"It was too cutthroat for my taste."

"That was not the answer I was expecting." Tina actually laughed, relaxing back into the conversation. It was the strangest thing. She never relaxed in conversation, especially not with a man, not that she had much or any experience in that regard.

"What did you think I would say? That math was too hard?"

To probably both their surprise, Tina laughed again.

"Well, math *is* hard. But after witnessing you throw a football with my son until you both had sore shoulders, I wouldn't have thought cutthroat would be a deterrent for you."

His answering chuckle did inexplicable things to Tina's insides, and she almost dropped the phone that she held pressed tightly to her ear. Or rather it had previously been pressed tightly but now she was too distracted by the long-forgotten sensations brought on by a handsome man's deep laughter in her ear.

"I can see why you would think that, I suppose. And you're right that I don't mind some good-natured competition. But cutthroat is a whole other level and not one I had expected or was prepared for. I lasted a decade, though, before I had to cash out. I just couldn't see myself spending my life always pursuing the next deal at that level of intensity." He paused for a moment. Tina was surprised by his heavy sigh. "It also felt dishonest. There's something so reassuringly honest about construction."

"The number of bodies they've found in concrete might argue differently," Tina countered.

"I'm fairly sure that only happens in cheap cop shows," Clark argued with another chuckle. "Or, I suppose, I should just say I've never come across any body parts. I put in my sweat and effort, and a house or deck or shed or whatever comes out at the end. Very honest, to my mind."

"It must be nearly as physically challenging and risky as football," Tina remarked. "You haven't come terribly far since your school days after all."

"I guess I haven't," Clark agreed without rancor. "Did you always want to be a vet? And are you happy with that choice?"

"I am, yes. I briefly thought about being an astronaut, but yeah, I pretty much always wanted to be a veterinarian. I wasn't allowed to have pets as a child, so that made me all the more determined to be surrounded by them as an adult. But now that I *am* an adult, I can understand why my parents didn't want pets in the house. At the moment, Tyler and I only have one very independent cat. I don't even really consider myself to be a cat person if one had to choose."

"I'd picture you more as a llama person," Clark said in a cheerful voice that forced another chuckle from Tina.

"Why's that? Because they look so cute but then they spit at you?"

Her quick response made Clark laugh, and soon they were both lost in gales of laughter. He didn't counter her words, though, so they were likely at least somewhat true. She could understand why he would think that, and he was probably right. Tina tried not to sigh when she was able to get her laughter under control. She didn't want to sound dramatic or hysterical. The level of laughter might seem a little crazy when all the circumstances were taken into consideration. But it was a perfect release of all her pent-up tension. She ought to let Clark go. Not that he seemed eager or even inclined to get off the phone. But she didn't want to muddy these particular waters. He was here to be a mentor to Tyler. That was the most important thing. That was the only reason she was even making an effort to be pleasant to him.

She was slightly jarred by her reluctance to end the conversation. And therefore was all the more motivated to do so.

"Thanks for your understanding, Clark. We'll see you tomorrow at the beach again, then?"

"I'm looking forward to it. Ten o'clock?"

"See you then."

Tina didn't tell him that she was looking forward to it too because she wondered if she was losing her mind. How could she be looking forward to seeing him again? Just that afternoon she had questioned whether or not he had abducted her son or worse. Now she was looking forward to spending time with him and almost eager to send her only child into his company?

She ought to ask her parents if there were any instances of mental illness in the family trees.

But she had been right to look forward to their time with Clark. Tyler loved running around behind a ball with the man, and Tina was actually able to relax enough to see the words on the pages of the book she had brought, even if the story still wasn't making complete sense to her.

Tina wasn't sure if she would ever be completely comfortable with the situation. Having another adult in Tyler's life wasn't something she had ever anticipated. Especially not someone she had just met. Her childhood friends were people she trusted down to the soles of her feet. Strangers were never welcome in her life unless they were pet parents but then that was a purely professional relationship. She didn't know what to call the relationship they were developing with Clark.

"I'm open, I'm open," Tyler yelled, waving his hands over his head as though Clark couldn't see him.

Tina had to bite her lip to not laugh out loud. They were at the beach once more, their favorite one, of course. Clark and Tyler were playing some sort of game Tina was sure they had made up with one of Clark's workmates and his son. Tina was starting to think she ought to let Clark take Tyler on his own rather than her accompanying them every time. But she had really started to enjoy spending time either the three of them or as a spectator of the two of them, and she was loath to give it up even though that was the original plan.

But she really ought to. She was going to, she assured herself. In fact, she would talk to Clark about it when they were finished that afternoon. Tina returned her attention to the book she still hadn't finished reading. If it had been a veterinary journal, she probably would have devoured it within a day or two of having received it. What was it about fiction that she just couldn't get into it?

With a shake of her head, Tina hardened her resolve. The author of the book had given her friend Rachel a big assist in getting her own writing career off the ground. Tina was determined to show her support by completing the reading of her recent release even if it took her the entire summer. It obviously wouldn't come to that. If she stopped following Tyler and Clark around, she would have some undivided attention to devote to the book.

Tina shook her head again while trying not to laugh at her own absurdity. Perhaps, rather than a silly novel, she ought to start reading more books about the various changes she was trying to make like nutrition, fitness, communication, and positivity. While they might be just as challenging to get through, at least they would be improving rather than just a story.

Her attention drifted once more as she pondered why she didn't enjoy reading fiction. Tyler loved it. She was forever taking him to the library. She was relieved that they could go during the week now that he was off school, and she had cut back on her hours at work so that they could avoid the crowds. It was probably as simple as the fact that she had read regularly to Tyler when he was a baby ,but she couldn't remember her parents reading to her as a child.

"How's your book coming along?" Clark asked as he sank down beside her to down a bottle of water while the two boys and the other boy's dad went to splash in the waves. "Isn't that the same book you've been reading since I met you?" His laughter turned to a frown. "Since I know you graduated, I'm sure you must be literate. Do you have a problem with your vision?"

Tina was further convinced that she was on the way to turning over the leaves she was working on when she was able to laugh at his question rather than taking offense. "Not that I know of. I'm just not really into reading novels, I'm afraid. But I sort of know the author, so I keep trying." She tossed the book away from her on the blanket she was stretched upon. "What about you? Do you read much fiction?"

Clark shrugged. "I do, actually. I'd rather read than watch television most of the time. Unless it's a good cop show." He scratched his head. "Do you think it's the genre? From the looks of that cover, it's not really what I would say I could picture you reading."

Tina laughed. "What do you think I should be reading?"

"Well *should* is a pretty strong word, but I could recommend you some books," he offered. "Actually, I could lend you some the next time we go out."

"About that," Tina began, feeling a cramp of nerves forming in her stomach. "I was just thinking that I ought to let you and Tyler start going on your own. I realized I've already decided I trust you at least a week or two ago, and I just keep tagging along because I've grown accustomed to it. But that wasn't the original agreement, so I should stop hovering."

Clark's frown returned. "You don't have to stop coming with us. I've gotten used to you being around, too. Won't Tyler find it weird if you stop coming with us?"

Tina reached a hand out to touch his forearm and instantly regretted it when a wave of warmth encompassed her. She was proud of herself for her restraint in not snatching it back again immediately.

"I should have stopped after the first couple of visits. It would have been less weird then. But I have a feeling he'll barely notice my absence." When Clark went to protest, Tina took the opportunity to regain possession of her hand, waving it between them as though to wave away his words. "I'm not saying my son doesn't love me nearly as much as I love him, but he has so much fun with you, I suspect he might even have more without being under my watchful gaze."

Clark looked less delighted by her words than she would have expected, but she tried not to be carried away by how gratifying she found that to be.

He cleared his throat. "Well then, I'll lend you a book or two when I pick him up from you, in that case," he finally said with a bashful dip of his head.

"I look forward to seeing which books you think I'll enjoy," Tina replied with a laugh before they were interrupted by Tyler's arrival, seeking his own bottle of water.

"It's the strangest experience of my life, in some ways," Tina was explaining to Angela weeks later.

"I know, hun, but you seem much more relaxed about the whole thing. In fact, I would say you're much more relaxed in general. Do you think you were unconsciously stressed about Tyler and your solely feminine influence upon him? Were you worried you weren't providing him enough balance?"

"Are you trying to shrink my head, Doctor Angela?" Tina asked with a laugh.

"Even this, you've changed," Angela pointed out with a grin and a gentle lift of her wine glass. "I like it," she added lest Tina take offense.

"You still love me, though, right?" Tina asked, only half joking. She didn't even recognize herself half the time, she wasn't certain how anyone else perceived her.

"Tina!" Angela burst out in exasperation. "You've been my best friend since we were in kindergarten. I will love you no matter what. I loved you when you got all weird and cranky. I'll continue to love you if you get a little less cranky, I can assure you."

Tina laughed but it was forced. She knew she had been a wretched shrew for years. She couldn't help it. She had probably always had a tendency toward the sarcastic, but ever since Karl she hadn't been able to control the bitterness that pervaded her entire being. Except in her dealings with Tyler. He was her heart and soul, and she would do anything for that boy, including turn herself inside out. She supposed she could consider herself Exhibit A of that inside out situation she had thought of. But she didn't need her best friend's comments on the topic, even though she had asked for them.

Angela must have realized she had taken her reassurance too far as she reached forward and rubbed Tina's shoulder in what ought to have been a comforting gesture. Tina was such a jumble inside nothing was as it ought to be.

"When does Tyler see Clark again?"

Tina sighed. "They're going camping," she said glumly. "This weekend," she added.

"And you aren't tagging along," Angela added with understanding dawning on her features. "So, you're freaking out a little bit, right?"

Tina grinned and nodded despite the freaking out part. "You've got that right," she said with emphasis.

"But you trust Clark, right?"

"Well, I must or I'd never let Tyler out of my sight with him. But I probably should have let them do something without me that didn't involve overnight. I might have been a little more sane about the whole thing in that case."

"Or maybe not," Angela said with a giggle. "You'll never be comfortable letting Tyler out of your sight. Not until he's in his twenties, at least."

"Ugh! I hope you're wrong. It's ridiculous. I'm ridiculous." Tina nearly wailed that last statement.

"No, you're not. Tyler has been solely your responsibility since before he was even born. Your feelings are completely valid and understandable. You are not being ridiculous."

Tina smiled at her friend to show her appreciation. Even if Angela didn't have all the details, Tina appreciated that she was behind her either way.

"Thanks, Ang."

"So, what do you have planned to help you cope?"

"I was thinking about a pint of chocolate chip ice cream," Tina admitted.

"No way, look how far you've come. You look like you've lost at least fifteen pounds. You can't undo that just because of a few stressful emotions."

Tina grinned and nodded. "Seventeen pounds, actually."

"There you go. No ice cream. Next option," she demanded.

Tina laughed. "Well, there are some chick flicks I was thinking of binging. I don't like to inflict those on Tyler, so I thought now would be a good time to catch up on them."

Angela nodded. "That sounds far healthier. You can always come over here and get a dose of kids if you get really lonely."

Tina laughed again, feeling shockingly light-hearted on the topic, despite her various fears about it.

"I just can't wait to hear how he feels about camping, you know? It's something he's always wanted to do but I've never wanted to invest in for so many reasons. But Clark already had all the stuff. All Tyler needs to take is his sleeping bag and one of my yoga mats so he's not sleeping directly on the ground." She paused and huffed a breath of air. "I do hope it's as awesome as he's always hoped. But I kind of dread the thought that I'm going to have to invest in all the gear if he really loves it."

Angela shrugged. "Or you can just leave it to Clark to take him."

Tina nodded dubiously. "What if Clark loses interest in Tyler, though? I mean, I'm not sure how long he intends to be committed to this relationship or arrangement, or whatever you'd call what he has going on with Tyler. If he moves away or starts a family of his own, I'm going to be back to trying to fill these roles for Tyler."

"You sure do like to borrow trouble, don't you?"

Tina huffed a laugh and shrugged. "I wouldn't put it that way, but I can see why you would say so." Tina tossed back the last of the wine in her glass with a slight slurp. "I don't know, Ang, I'm such a mess. I wonder if losing a few pounds is really going to make enough of a difference to my psyche that I can be an almost normal human."

"It's not our weight that makes us normal, my dear," Angela pointed out in a reasonable tone that just about set Tina's teeth on edge.

"I know that. But I'm hoping feeling good about myself might do the trick."

"Why don't you feel good about yourself? Is it something to do with your husband?" she asked, surprising Tina with her perception. "You never talk about him, but I always knew you shouldn't have gone to a different school than me."

Tina ignored her friend's question, leaning into the second part of what she said instead.

"They didn't offer enough medical courses at your school for me to be able to get into veterinary school."

"That's a ridiculous statement considering the fact that I studied psychology."

"You might have studied psychology, but that's pretty much all book learning, isn't it?"

Angela rolled her eyes. "You aren't going to look down your nose at my degree, now, are you?"

Tina laughed and shook her head. "That would only further prove the point of what I'm trying to change."

The rest of the evening passed in gentle camaraderie leaving Tina to wonder why all relationships couldn't be so comfortable.

Chapter Seventeen

"**H**ow happy is your mom going to be to see us, do you think?"

Clark had enjoyed his weekend away with Tyler so much he had realized why Doctor Tina had been so afraid of their association. He actually felt reluctant to return the kid. Not that he would actually ever consider stealing someone's child, but Clark certainly wished he had a son of his own. A ten-year-old boy is the best, he thought with a pang.

His mother was right. He should have started his family years ago.

But he had been too busy making his millions. A fat lot of good those millions were doing him now. Yeah, he could buy whatever he wanted, but where was the fun in that if no one else could do the same with him? And sitting around drinking beer just made you fat and boring. It got old way faster than people thought. And so here he was living on this small-town island taking someone else's kid for a camping trip.

But the borrowed boy was pleasant company and they had enjoyed their time in the woods even more than Clark had anticipated. If he could get them home before the vet's requested curfew, he might even be allowed to do it again. But the ferry was taking longer than usual to dock, and they were going to be cutting it close. Clark sent another text message.

Might be a few mins late.

Sorry. Docking problems.

Clark felt as though he was all thumbs whenever he tried texting with Tyler's mom. He wasn't sure what it was about the woman that made him feel so insecure, but it was probably a combination of her superior attitude and her beauty that made him feel like a bumbling adolescent with his first crush.

He should so not be crushing on his mentee's mom. That was just asking for trouble. And yet here he was holding his breath waiting for her to reply to his text.

I understand.

Do you want me to meet you somewhere to save you time?

Clark liked that she didn't ever abbreviate her text messages. It made him laugh, but he quite liked that silly quality. He didn't think she was very old, certainly not older than him, but she often struck him like a little old lady. That shouldn't be an attractive quality to a man of thirty-six, but here they were.

No problem. Will bring Ty home straight away.

Thank you! I can't wait to see him.

Clark could just imagine how much she must have missed the kid. Tyler truly was a fantastic boy. Clark was going to miss him through the week after a great two days of hiking, camping, and fishing. He might not miss the boy's unending questions, though. The hardest one to deal with was when he had asked Clark if he would consider marrying his mom.

How was he supposed to answer a question like that?

"Uh, well, I don't know your mom very well," he'd managed to stammer out.

"You could get to know her," Tyler pointed out. "She's really great. Especially once you get to know her," he'd added with an open, guileless face, so eager that Clark's urge to laugh had died quickly in his throat.

"She'd have to be pretty great to make you so awesome," Clark had agreed but quickly regretted it when Tyler's face brightened further.

"So, you'll at least think about it?"

Clark had to laugh at that point. It was such a parental thing to say. 'I'll think about it.' Clark could remember his mother saying that whenever she didn't want to say *no* right off the bat. But he didn't want to make the boy any promises he couldn't keep. He didn't have any intention of thinking about it.

"Your mom might not appreciate you playing matchmaker."

"I don't know what that means," Tyler had replied, making Clark laugh again. "But I really think she could use a husband, and I know I need a dad, so it could be perfect, don't you think?"

What could he say after that?

Clark had changed the subject back to the s'mores they were making at the moment and had intended to not give it further thought. But now here he was remembering the conversation and thinking about the possibilities.

Tyler was nearly asleep in the backseat. It was weird for Clark to have to put the boy back there, but laws were laws. Until he was twelve, he couldn't ride in the front. Clark hadn't wanted to take a chance even though he was reasonably sure the boy was tall enough that the airbag wasn't an issue. But it was too big a risk to take. He would never forgive himself if something happened to Tyler. And he was more than one hundred percent certain Tyler's mom would never forgive him either.

Clark was, in fact, almost shocked Tina had allowed them to go on this camping trip. It seemed the sort of thing she would be terrified of. But she had agreed with only a little bit of resistance. Clark had framed it as a celebration of Tyler's finishing fifth grade. He would be going into middle school next year.

He was all the happier that they had found one another. Middle school years were the worst ones in life. The ones in which a kid needed all the resources possibly available to him. In Tyler's case, he needed to keep Clark in his life.

And Clark already knew he needed the kid in his life. There was just something so fulfilling about having a boy to care about. He could only hope he was giving as much as he got out of the relationship.

Even having to coordinate with the cranky veterinarian was worth the hassle if it meant being friends with her son. And probably the boy was so great mostly because of his mom. That ought to warm him up towards Tina. And it did. But to consider marrying her? Why did his heart actually kick into gear at the thought? It should be a laughable thought, not one that felt meaningful and worth considering.

"Welcome home, buddy," Clark said in a loud whisper as he pulled into Tyler's driveway, causing the boy to mumble and stir behind him.

"Are we there already?" Tyler asked, confused.

Tina must have been watching out the window for them as she was by the car before it even came to a complete stop. A surprisingly wide grin was stretching her face as her eyes seemed to devour every detail of her son. Clark loved that about her.

What? Loved? What a ridiculous word to use even in his own thoughts. He didn't love anything about the woman. Admired made far more sense. It was commendable that she so obviously adored her son. That was right and normal and good. She was a good mom. He admired that about her. That was all.

Why did Tyler have to plant such a crazy idea in his brain?

Clark only hoped he could be normal for the few minutes it would take to unload Tyler and his few belongings.

"How was it? Did you catch many fish? Thank you for your messages, Clark, I appreciated seeing a few pictures while you were away."

"Did he send you the big one, Mom?" Tyler asked excitedly before Clark could respond to Tina's expressions of gratitude.

Clark stood and watched while mother and son interacted. Tina had changed. He wasn't sure how exactly to describe it. Maybe softened was the right word. She had been extremely hard and sharp when they'd first met.

It was quite odd because he was pretty sure she was trying to get in shape. It often happened that women became harder in mind or personality as they did so in body but with Tina, it seemed to be the opposite. He wondered absently what sort of stress she carried in her life that this would be the case. Because he suspected that was the difference. She seemed a little more relaxed. Relaxed wasn't a word one would use to describe her if you had just met, he didn't think. But since he had met her a couple months previously, he supposed she had relaxed, at least a fraction.

He wondered if it was that she had grown accustomed to him or if she had relaxed in other

163

aspects of her life as well. Tina didn't strike him as the sort who enjoyed change or new people so maybe she had just accepted him into her life now. That might explain the difference.

But she had certainly gotten into shape. He could see clear differences in her.

He shouldn't be looking. Tyler's mom was off limits, despite the boy's request that he consider marrying his mother. It would surely mess with the arrangements he had with the school if he were to become involved with the mother of his mentee.

And he deeply enjoyed his position as mentor to the ten-year-old boy. Clark would never want to do anything that would put that in jeopardy. Even if the boy's mom was turning out to be a ten.

Clark dragged his attention back to the present. The way both Tina and Tyler were looking at him told him they were expecting a response to a question he couldn't recall hearing.

"I'm sorry, I must have zoned out for a second. I didn't realize I was so tired."

Instantly Tina was full of sympathetic concern, again not something Clark would have expected from her. "You had to do all the driving, didn't you?" she asked, or rather stated. "Were you able to sleep much while camping or were the woods too noisy at night?"

"I slept like a log," Tyler declared before Clark could answer but despite Tina looking at her son briefly with a grin, she kept her focus on Clark.

"I was far more aware of the surroundings than I usually am," Clark admitted, allowing his gaze to flicker toward Tyler, causing a sympathetic sound to erupt from Tina's throat.

"I suppose you were on the lookout, weren't you? I would have been the same for multiple reasons, which is one of the many reasons why I am happy that you were willing to take Tyler on his first camping expedition. While I have an appreciation for the outdoors, I have no interest in moving into it, even on a temporary basis."

Clark chuckled over the dramatic shudder she exhibited with her words. Before he could reply, though, she continued speaking.

"What we were asking you is if you wanted to stay for supper or if you had to get home right away, seeing as it's Sunday."

"I wouldn't want to put you to any trouble," Clark began.

"It's just pizza and salad. I already made both, so no trouble at all."

He ought to say no. No good could come of him letting her into his life. It would be terrible to let Tyler get his hopes up. And yet, rather than declining, he heard, "Well, then in that case, I'd be happy to stay, thank you," coming out of his mouth, and he almost clamped a hand over it to stem the words. But that would have been even more ridiculous. They were already out of his mouth. And what could a few more minutes in their company hurt?

They could hurt a lot as it turned out.

Clark didn't want to leave.

He was the world's biggest idiot.

What was so special about a slightly crusty, trying to get in shape, highly intelligent, single mother? Why did he enjoy their company so immensely? Why was everything Tyler said so completely enthralling? Why did he want to stay planted on their sofa while Tyler scampered off to get his bath? It took considerable effort for him to get the words out of his mouth, but he made them come anyway.

"Thank you for the supper, I had a great time."

She opened her mouth and then closed it again as though she had changed her mind about what she was going to say. Clark wondered if she was feeling even an increment of what he was going through. Had she been about to ask him to stay longer and then thought better of it? Or was she on the opposite spectrum and hoping he would hurry up and leave?

That thought got him to his feet faster than anything else could.

"I wish we could do something more to repay your kindness," was what she finally said as she trailed him toward the door.

He wouldn't leave without saying goodbye to Tyler, but it was better if he was ready to go as soon as he'd done that. Especially if all she had to offer him was gratitude. He ought to be happy about her gratitude since she had been so hard to deal with before, but contrarily, now he wanted more from her.

He was a moron.

"Spending time with Tyler is reward enough, I can assure you," Clark answered her when he could get his thoughts in order. "You've got one of the best kids I've ever met."

Her entire face softened, and a sweet smile spread across it gently. "Thank you so much for saying that, Clark. I often think that, but I know I'm biased, so it's wonderful to hear someone else say it." She laughed then, sounding self-conscious. "It's not bragging to think that, is it?"

"A little bragging isn't going to hurt anyone," he pointed out with a laugh. "And as long as you don't say it out loud to the other moms of kids his age you should be fine."

She laughed too, and the rich sound caught at his belly doing weird things to him. He needed to leave. He couldn't catch any sort of feelings for this woman. Why was Tyler's bath taking him so long?

"Do you have to start work really early in the morning?" Tina asked, prolonging the conversation but returning to safe topics.

"It's our normal time, but you might think it's early," Clark replied with a wink that he immediately regretted. He couldn't be flirtatious with her. But he liked being flirtatious. He never should have accepted the supper invitation. "Seven o'clock is our meet up time, usually, on every jobsite. We don't usually start making much noise until eight. But we like to make sure we're all set and ready to go as soon as the clock strikes eight."

"The neighbors of your jobsites must love that."

Clark shrugged. "They would hate it more if we started at seven."

Tina laughed slightly. "True, but they'd hate it less if you waited until nine for the noise."

Clark shrugged again. "We'd never be able to finish a job if we waited. With how hot it can get after noon, we can't work at all some days. With such a small window to get stuff done, we need to do what we need to do."

Tina nodded with a frown. "I never really thought about that," she answered honestly. "It's an even harder job than I realized. Do you ever miss your office job?"

"Nope," Clark answered shortly but in a cheerful tone. He didn't want to discuss it. With anyone, not just her. That was a very closed chapter in his life. The only thing he wanted to keep from that time period was his ability to properly invest his own money. Well, that and the nest egg he had saved up.

Did men use that word? He liked it. He wanted a nest to feather. A family of his own to provide for and spoil. Maybe he wouldn't bother working anymore if he had a family to spend time with. For now, the guys he worked with were pretty much his family. Of course, he still had his brothers and their families. And his mom, too. But they were all wrapped up in their own lives. They didn't want him trying to manage them anymore. It was as it should be, but it had hurt nonetheless. He was having fun here on the Cape and trying to make a full life for himself. Tyler was a part of that. But Tina couldn't be, lest he mess it up.

Finally, after what felt like an eon but was probably only ten or fifteen minutes, Tyler scampered back into the room and Clark could take his leave.

"Hey, Bud, I thought you were going to wash all your skin completely off, you were in there for so long."

Tina's sharp glance told him that maybe it hadn't been that long after all. Tyler didn't take offense, though, only shrugging and laughing.

"Thanks again for such a great weekend, Clark. I really loved everything about it. If you ever feel like going again, I'll be really glad to go with you."

"I will definitely keep that in mind," Clark answered with a laugh. He was so convoluted in his feelings at the moment that he wasn't about to make any promises. "I really enjoyed it, too." And then he went and violated his own wishes. "Next time we'll have to try rough camping."

He wanted to be mad at himself for referring to a next time but what would be the point? There would definitely be a next time. And Tyler's delight was worth it.

"What's rough camping?" Tyler asked eagerly.

"Where you go into the woods and spend time in the rough, like in a national forest or federal lands, rather than in a campground. It's much more primitive but feels very rewarding if you can still have a good time."

Tyler appeared eager, but Tina's expression was dubious.

"And you think this would be fun?" she asked, her tone indicating she didn't agree.

Clark laughed but before he could answer Tyler was explaining how awesome it would be.

"Imagine, Mom, you can pit yourself against nature and win."

"What if nature wins, though, Ty?"

"She won't," the boy answered with full confidence, making even his worried mother smile.

"We'll have to try fishing and hiking a little bit more before we try rough camping."

Tyler nodded eagerly.

"But you have school tomorrow, so I should get myself gone so you can go to bed."

Before he could take his leave, though, Tyler crashed into him with his arms stretched around his waist. Clark's heart lodged itself in his throat and he returned the boy's hug.

"Thank you, Clark. I had the best time of my life," Tyler said into his belly. Clark's gaze lifted to Tina's, but she didn't seem the least bit offended. In fact, she appeared delighted by the development, much to his shock. He would have thought she'd be angry that the best moment of her son's life wasn't spent with her. But then, she hadn't wanted to consider trying to camp, so he supposed she was relieved to be let off that particular hook.

"Goodnight, Clark, drive safe," she called to him after he was able to peel himself away from Tyler and leave the house.

It took effort to make himself leave. Tina's house held what Clark wanted for himself. A ready-made family. It might make sense for a man to want to start a family of his own, fresh, but there was just something about Tina and Tyler that made Clark want to join in and make them a trio.

Of course, that would carry complications he clearly wasn't thinking of at the moment. And Tina would most likely not be on board for him rearranging her life. Clark was being an idiot to even entertain the idea. But he couldn't help himself.

It was probably the fatigue. Maybe after a good night's sleep and a busy week, he'd have his head on straight.

Chapter Eighteen

Tina could only hope she didn't have a goofy expression on her face. Her too perceptive son would notice and might even come to the right conclusion. She didn't need Tyler trying to play matchmaker any more than he already had from time to time in his young life.

"Goodnight, Mom," was all he said, though, and even that was garbled around the huge yawn he didn't even try to suppress.

"Sweet dreams, Tyler," Tina said as she watched him walk to his room. She hadn't left her spot against the door where she had wilted to after closing it on Clark's retreating back.

How could she enjoy the man's company? He was a neanderthal. Wasn't he? She didn't want to be attracted to any man, but if she was going to lose her mind and do so, why couldn't it be some nice, studious, quiet guy who she could play scrabble with or something? Not this macho, tough guy who plays football and throws hammers. He would never see anything in her. Not that she would want him to, of course.

But he *was* dreamy. His face and voice were enough to set her belly to fluttering in a way it hadn't done since she was in college. Not since she'd become serious with Karl.

She had fallen hard for Karl, nearly at first glance. They had met during her first year of college. It was his second year, so he had seemed so much older and more mature than she and her classmates were. That had been part of his appeal. Also, his accent. He had sounded so intelligent.

It had turned out to all be a façade, of course. He hadn't been the wise, loving man she had thought he was. It had taken her way too long to realize that. She had no intention of reliving any of that experience. She had proven to herself that her judgment was less than poor.

What could be less than poor? Abysmal? Dreadful? Hurtful?

However you worded it, when it came to men, Tina had bad judgment. She couldn't take that sort of risk while Tyler was young, even if she was willing to take a risk for herself. She had learned that bruises heal but emotional wounds do not. She was still marked from her experience. Tina didn't really want to risk it for herself, either, but she would do anything to protect her son. That included not allowing anyone into his life who might hurt him.

She now trusted Clark enough to know he wouldn't hurt Tyler. But there was the chance of Tyler's pain if his mother were to be hurt. The relationship between a man and a woman was of course far different from that of a man and a boy. It was far more fragile. If she were to form a relationship with Clark and it ended, where would that leave Tyler?

Why was she even thinking about this?

Tina scoffed at herself and pushed herself away from the door that she was *still* leaning against like a lunatic.

She did not have the hots or even the warms for Clark. He was nothing to her except her son's mentor. For that mentorship, she was truly grateful. That was it. End of story. There were no more thoughts to be had for the handsome man.

Even that descriptor had to end. He was a nice person. That's it. No other descriptors were allowed.

Tina tried to convince herself and thought she had done so. Except she dreamt about him through the night. Romantic sorts of thoughts and dreams. Not at all the "nice person, end of story" thoughts.

Waking up, feeling uncertain of how refreshed she was, Tina refused to think about the thoughts or dreams she'd had. It was another busy week ahead of her. Tyler's last week of school and her last week at full capacity at the veterinary clinic.

It was one more of the new things she was trying. She had notified all her patients' owners that she would be reducing her hours in the summer and that routine checkups would be best scheduled before the middle of June. It had worked well. She had been extra busy throughout the spring, but now there were almost no bookings for the summer. She would be on call for emergencies but mostly her receptionist and assistant would look after as much as they could. She was excited to see what fun she and Tyler could get up to throughout the summer.

But she had one very busy week to get through first.

She tried not to allow her thoughts to dwell excessively on the summer. Tina didn't consider herself to be a fun sort of person. She had been far too intense and up tight since Karl to be fun or light-hearted. But it was time to try.

She had already proven she could play. She had always followed Tyler's lead in that regard. He was a delightful boy who didn't seem to be scarred by his genetics nor by his slightly inept mother. She was the most fortunate of women in that department.

Where would the summer take them?

Not now, Tina, she admonished herself as she greeted a pleasant Golden Retriever named Max and his stressed-out owner Bev. The dog's declining health kept her occupied for the next thirty minutes and beyond. Tina wasn't sure Max would make it through the summer. That would be a drag for both Max and Bev, but also for Tina. She tried hard not to get attached to her patients, but it wasn't always easy. Max had been one of her first patients when she had opened her clinic, and she loved him nearly as much as Bev did.

Perhaps she and Tyler should consider another pet. Poor old Maisie wasn't going to last forever and didn't provide much if any companionship. This summer would be the ideal time to deal with training one. Especially if they were to get a dog. Tyler would be thrilled, of course, but then, she had to consider the facts of the end of summer arriving and how the poor dog would cope with their return to their regular routines. There was always the option of her taking a pet to work with her.

Tina sighed. Clearly, she was turning into a different person. Tyler had been asking her for a pet for years, and she had always said no. She almost didn't recognize herself anymore. Not just the physical, although her now nearly twenty-pound weight loss was starting to really show in her face and everywhere else, but it wasn't just that. It was something in her eyes. She was losing her cynical edge.

She wasn't sure how she felt about that.

She was reasonably sure not being a grouchy wretch made her a better person. But her crabby, cynical crust had saved her from a lot of pain over the past decade.

It might have also prevented other people from getting close to her, but Tina wasn't sure if that was a good or bad thing. She would take it under advisement, she told herself with a laugh that was another new aspect to her personality. When had she started to laugh so much?

She refused to think that it was having Clark in their lives.

Rather, perhaps it was just that she was now strong enough to not require the crust, so her subconscious had decided to allow it to dissipate. That was a much better explanation to Tina's way of thinking. She might not mind being a little less of a grouch, but she certainly wasn't ready to jump into any sort of boy-girl relationship.

Clark Stevens was merely her son's mentor.

Merely wasn't the right word, though. It was a big deal. Tyler loved that man, and even Tina could admit that the relationship was doing her son good. She wanted to think she had done an excellent job of raising Tyler, and she knew that wasn't just her own bias speaking. She had managed to keep her own issues from rubbing off on the boy, at least for the most part. But she could see that he held himself differently. He had always been a happy kid, but it seemed to her that he was even happier than he had ever been. Like somehow being able to do all the things he had always wished for but Tina hadn't been able to do fulfilled some sort of hole that had been missing in his life.

Tina refused to let that hurt her. She was only one person. She had done the best that she could, and the fact that Tyler was as awesome as he was testified to the fact that she had done a pretty good job. And then, when there was a requirement to do more, she had done what was necessary, as any good mom would. In this particular case, that had meant she needed to get over her own feelings about letting someone into their lives.

Not that she was allowing Clark into her life. Only Tyler's. She was safe.

Tina blinked down at the chihuahua she was examining. Her thoughts had clearly strayed far from the topic at hand. But when had her safety become a question? Clark was not a threat to her physical safety. She knew him well enough now to fully trust that.

But, she realized, it was her heart, her innermost person that she was guarding. That was why she had allowed herself to be a wretch these past ten years. If she didn't let anyone in, she couldn't be hurt. But what was that doing to her son? If she didn't let anyone into their lives, was she making his too small?

The small dog must have sensed her disquiet as he began to shiver and whine. She pushed her negative thoughts to the side while scratching the little quivering creature behind the ears.

"I'm ok, Tinkerbell, and so are you, I promise," she crooned gently as she probed the tumor she was supposed to be examining. From what she could tell, it was merely a cyst, but she would have to take a tissue sample to be certain. Tinkerbell wasn't going to enjoy the process.

"I'm not going to love it, either, I promise you. But not knowing isn't going to change facts. So, we have to face the reality, right?"

The little dog stared at her trustingly. It was the exact reason why she loved her job so much. Animals never bit you for no reason. They didn't have ulterior motives aside from their bellies. They were far better people than humans.

But she needed to stop limiting her son's life.

She was fortunate to have realized while Tyler was still young enough for her to start changing things. Tina's stomach cramped at the thought of trying to open themselves up to even more people, but it was probably time. They were strong enough now. Tyler had a voice, and she had raised him well. He was no longer a vulnerable infant. It was time.

And she wasn't a fragile twenty-three-year-old wide-eyed looking at the one person who'd sworn to love her forever as he raised a hand to demonstrate just how strong his feelings really were. They could do this.

"We're going to be just fine, little Bell," she promised the dog, meaning the both of them in that moment.

Chapter Nineteen

She tried to set her plan into action at a barbecue at Rachel and Jake's house a few days later. It was just their small group of Angela, her husband, their three kids, Evelyn and her husband from next door, and Tina and Tyler. Rachel was fairly recently returned to the Cape and still making friends herself, but Tina was reasonably sure the small selection was out of deference for her comfort rather than their hosts' choice. Although, after further thought, Tina couldn't imagine having any more people than that for a gathering, but she never threw parties and barbecues, so what did she know?

"So, I need to learn how to make friends."

She said it loud enough for the other women to hear her when it was only the four of them gathering around the salads and such. The men were hovering over the barbecue on the front covered deck, and the kids were down on the beach playing. It was the perfect time. But Tina hadn't expected the stunned silence that followed her words. She tried to explain herself.

"I haven't tried since college."

They still stared at her before Rachel broke the silence with a giggle.

"What do you call us?" Rachel asked with a gesture toward Evelyn and Angela.

"You don't count because we've been friends since childhood, and you brought Evelyn along on your own."

Tina didn't mean it to sound grouchy, but she recognized that she hadn't broken through her crust as much as she thought when she saw Evelyn visibly flinch from her words. Tina knew she had changed, though, when she immediately reached out to the other woman both literally and figuratively. She had never been the demonstrative sort. She probably ought to try to hug Evelyn. Instead, though, she grabbed one of her hands.

"That was not to say I don't consider you a friend, Evelyn, at all. I swear I do. And you can attest to that because I asked you for advice. Something you should know I haven't done since maybe even before college. But you made it so easy that I don't feel like I actually had anything to do with making our friendship, do you know what I mean? Like because you are so friendly and became friends with Rachel and then us just through association, I kind of feel like I didn't learn anything concrete from the experience."

The others were still looking at her as though they were shocked into silence. Tina sighed.

"I didn't think it would be so shocking that it would strike you ladies mute," she grumbled.

"It just seems a little out of character, is all, Tina," Angela explained with an almost nervous sounding chuckle. "What has brought this on?"

Tina shrugged. "I'm just realizing. For years I only had you, Ange. Then Rachel came back to town and joined us, because of you, not me. Then Evelyn joined through Rachel, again not anything to do with me. But I'm reasonably sure most people have more than three friends. You three have other friends than the rest of us, don't you?"

"They're more like acquaintances we spend time with sometimes," Rachel said with a laugh. Always so fond of words that she had to be precise. Tina laughed a little too but then shrugged.

"Well, I don't spend time with anyone other than you ladies and my parents. But I'm thinking Tyler might need more than that in his life. He needs to be as well rounded as I can possibly make him. I worry that I've been restricting him because of my own issues. And I've tried so very hard throughout his whole life not to do that."

Angela nodded. "You've done a wonderful job of that. No one would ever know you had so many hang-ups from looking at him."

Tina laughed and nodded. She couldn't argue with her friend's assessment.

"Does this have anything to do with Clark?" Evelyn asked, her perception surprising Tina.

Tina wasn't sure if it was because of Clark or not. She wasn't sure how to explain it, but she tried even though she started with a shrug and half a smile.

"I don't know. Probably at least a little. I felt forced to let him into our lives because of Tyler's request. But I can see that he is thriving under Clark's attention, so I can't regret it. So, yeah, I guess it does have to do with Clark. Seeing how much his attention is benefiting Tyler makes me wonder who else I should try to invite in."

Tina shook her head and sighed. "But I don't have the first clue where to even start."

The other women looked on in sympathetic silence as Tina's gaze returned to her son on the beach with Angela's children.

"I should have been friendlier with the parents of his classmates, probably. That would make sense as a way to start. But, ugh, they're not at all interesting to me. Am I the worst person on the planet for even thinking that?"

Evelyn, the peacekeeper in the group, reached out toward Tina to rub her arm in a gesture of comfort.

"Definitely not the worst, hun, but why do you think they aren't interesting? Have you even tried to get to know them at all? It might be a self-defence mechanism at work for you to think that. Maybe, are you afraid they aren't going to find you interesting for some reason and so you're projecting that feeling onto them?"

Angela laughed lightly from her side of the room. "You are starting to sound like a psychologist, Evie, but those are some valid questions."

"Whose side are you on?" Tina groused good-naturedly at Angela before turning back to Evelyn. "You might have a point. But it's scary to open myself up to potential criticism."

"But why would there be criticism? What do you think other people are going to judge you for?"

Tina huffed a frustrated breath as though she were irritated with the question, but she gazed up at the ceiling as though searching for the answer to Evelyn's question, or maybe to fight the threat of tears.

"I'm awfully young to be a single mother," she finally said in a smaller voice than usual.

"Actually, you aren't, sadly. Besides, what? You think someone would judge you for that? What do you think this is? 1950? You're a widow, for Pete's sake, not that you need to defend yourself."

Tina laughed over Rachel's outburst, but she appreciated the support more than the other woman could possibly know.

"But all the two-parent households can do more for their kid than I can."

"Like what?" Evelyn challenged. "What is Tyler lacking, besides a father, that you could give him with a two-parent household that he doesn't have now?"

"Well, more of my time, for one thing. More parental time means more mental stimulation, just ask Angela."

"That might be true, I wouldn't know as I'm not the one who studied psychology, but you have to know how great Tyler is. I can't imagine him being any more awesome than he already is. I think you're just projecting your own unearned sense of insecurity."

"Oh, I earned it all right," Tina said, thinking of her late husband. "But I appreciate what you're saying." She paused and looked out at Tyler once more. "So, you think I should try with the other parents?"

"How dismissive have you been in the past?" Angela asked. "Is that part of your hesitation, too?"

"You know me too well," Tina acknowledged. "I'd like to say I haven't been that dismissive, but I wouldn't really know, would I?"

Angela shook her head but then shrugged. "There's only one way to find out, isn't there?" She smiled encouragingly at Tina who only looked back blankly. "Give it a try, silly. Maybe linger over school drop offs or something."

"School just let out, though," Tina complained. "Just when I get the gumption and have the time."

"You should have a list of contact information for the parents of the other kids in his class. You could always call around on the premise of arranging playdates throughout the summer. Then you can see what sort of reception you get from the other parents. Maybe you'll be surprised and really hit it off with some of them." Angela smiled again before adding, "But I still don't think they have anything Tyler is missing."

"Thanks, friend," Tina said. "And I know what you mean about Tyler being such a great kid. But I still think he needs as much exposure as he can get if he's going to grow up to be a well-rounded adult. I mean, I'd like to think I know everything and I'm the best at everything, but let's be honest here –" she broke off with a laugh that her friends joined her in.

"You *are* the best," ever loyal Angela insisted firmly. "But I can see what you're saying about Tyler needing more contacts. I'm sorry you didn't have the best experience with the other parents, hun. Sometimes places where everyone is similar in one way breeds a competitive spirit. So, the kids are all the same age or in the same grade, they're peers, right? Somehow that makes the parents feel competitive on their child's behalf."

"That's kind of dumb," Tina said.

Angela nodded sadly. "True. But it's an explanation, not an excuse." Angela leaned forward and smacked her hands together with determination. "So, we need a plan. Your options are to either start with the school and go from there or start fresh somewhere else. Let's brainstorm friendship-sourcing ideas."

Evelyn laughed and joined the conversation again. "We might all need these ideas. I'm perfectly satisfied with having a small circle, but maybe I need more friends, too. I feel like Rachel said there are friends and then there are acquaintances you spend time with. What are you really looking for, Tina?"

Tina wrinkled her nose. "I guess I can see Rachel's point better now that we've discussed it. Like you said, I too am quite satisfied with my friend circle and don't really want to change it. But I would like to have access to other people so as to have potential possibilities for Tyler, you know what I mean?"

Evelyn nodded firmly. "That's a sound idea. So not to split hairs, but you're really wanting to know how to be more friendly rather than how to make friends. You obviously already know how to have friends. You have three right here, six if you count our husbands."

"Thanks Evie," Tina said with genuine gratitude. "And those are all I truly need."

"So how did you do with Clark? I know at first you were worried you might have scared him away with your concerns."

An almost chuckle escaped Tina. "Yeah, those were some times. Ugh. I was so worried about allowing Tyler to spend time with a stranger. Of course, there was all the background checks, but evil people can often hide their evilness. But it turns out he's a good guy." She paused for a moment. "But I think I was just fortunate enough that he was determined to stick to his commitment to Tyler, determined enough to put up with me. And I apologized regularly," she concluded with a laugh. "But I don't think random people are going to go along with that, do you?"

"Well, you also won't be coming from a place of terror, will you?" Angela pointed out reasonably. "So you aren't as likely to be on the offensive or even on the defensive. Just keep telling yourself you're looking at it as a sort of education." Angela looked around the group. "Maybe we should make it a project. We could all expand ourselves a little, couldn't we? And I, for the same reasons as Tina, really should do the same. I've been content, but Tina's right, the kids might need more. Let's all try to get to know one person this week, and we'll report back on our next girls' night."

"Speaking of girls' night," Rachel broke in, "We haven't had one of those in a while."

"I think it's my turn to host," Evelyn said with a giggle. "How about in ten days from now? Is midweek still ok for everyone? My husband will be out of town that night, so I'd love to have the company."

"Deal," Tina said with the widest grin she could remember gracing her face, despite the nerves jangling below the surface of her psyche. How was she going to make a new acquaintance?

She had gotten so used to ignoring everyone. It was going to take some effort. But she would always do what was necessary to benefit her son. There was no question about that. And surely, she wasn't too old to learn new things. She didn't believe that adage about dogs, she wouldn't believe it about herself either.

Chapter Twenty

Where to start, though?

That was the big question plaguing Tina's mind. She and the others had agreed they each had to get to know one person. They didn't have to become friends, just acquaintances. Or rather sufficient acquaintances that she could learn what that person had to offer her son.

When worded like that, she sounded dreadfully selfish. Was she willing to give back to the person that she thought she might exploit at some point for the benefit of her child? That was the soul-searching question she was still contemplating when she and Tyler met Clark at the beach one afternoon.

"I hope you don't mind my tagging along," Tina said to Clark as soon as he came into view. "I won't cramp your style, I promise. I just need to get out of the house and thought a long walk on the beach would do me good."

Clark's grin flipped her stomach, but Tina ignored the ridiculous reaction.

"You're always welcome, of course," he said with a pleasant smile that quickly turned into a frown. "But what has you so jittered up that you couldn't rest easy at home?"

"Well, this summer is the first time in my adult life that I actually have time on my hands, for one thing. It has been great in many ways, but I'm starting to think I don't have enough going on in my life."

"And your soul searching is making you anxious?"

Tina laughed and shrugged. "Something like that," she agreed. She watched as Tyler shook Clark's hand in a very mature fashion before tugging him toward the beach.

"Come on, Clark, you promised to show me a spiral again today."

Clark laughed and started to follow the boy before he glanced over his shoulder toward Tina. "Maybe we can talk a bit more about it later?"

Tina smiled, nodded, and waved, although she wasn't sure if she was willing to bare her innermost thoughts to the man. Besides, he was already her acquaintance, so he wouldn't count for the challenge.

With a shake of her head at herself, Tina gathered the few beach supplies she and Tyler had brought and carried them to a protected spot on the beach. Making sure Clark and Tyler noted where she was leaving everything, she set off at a brisk pace away from the two guys.

It was a surprise and almost a revelation to Tina to realize that she fully trusted Clark with her son. She had no qualms about walking away for a while. If only she could leave her turbulent thoughts behind just as easily.

How does one stop being so fiercely self-protective? That was the big question she had to find the answer to.

Tina was well aware of why she was the way that she was. The question was whether or not she was interested in changing the way that she was.

The hard shell she had erected around herself had served Tina well at the end of her brief marriage and after her husband walked out on her while she was pregnant and then killed himself in a fiery car crash. Being crusty had kept others at arm's length long enough for her open emotional wounds to heal enough that they went unnoticed for the most part. People just thought she was a cranky wench, they didn't think it through further than that as to why she had suddenly become far more acerbic than she had ever been. Most, if they thought about it at all, just attributed it to her grieving process.

She did, of course, grieve for Karl. She wasn't a total monster. But it was mostly grief over what could have been. If he hadn't changed so drastically, or if she hadn't been so wrong in her assessment of him, one or the other. She had thought they were deeply in love. She had thought they would remain that way forever. She had been very wrong.

And he hadn't wanted the baby.

That had been the part that broke Tina. While it was true that the pregnancy was unplanned, she didn't consider it unwanted. They were married! Shouldn't they want children as a result of that union?

One of Karl's arguments had been that they were too young. But that hadn't stopped him from wanting to marry her. Of course, in hindsight Tina knew that was only because she wouldn't sleep with him otherwise. But if they were old enough for all of that, they ought to be old enough to bear the consequences.

She tried to shrug off the heavy burden these thoughts were placing on her shoulders. She would never want Tyler to know that his father had been such a brute.

Karl hadn't hit her until at least six months into their marriage. She had been deep into her last year of studies and couldn't do everything. He wanted her to be Suzie Homemaker as well as get her studies done. She wasn't sure why he was so aggressive about it. It wasn't like she was asking him to pay her tuition. In fact, as it turned out, she had been stuck with paying for his due to the way they had consolidated their loans.

Years later, and with much more maturity and distance from the experience, besides years of listening to Angela talk psyche issues, Tina was reasonably sure Karl was disappointed with his own life. But the attacks had felt deeply personal at the time. And had damaged any sweetness she might have had within her. But she had protected her baby when Karl had tried to damage him. That was all that mattered.

And then Karl was gone.

And the only lies she had ever told her son were in connection to that loss. No one knew Karl was on that road because he was leaving Tina. It was understood that he was going to visit his parents. No one ever questioned the amount of luggage he had in the car with him. Tina had been too shocked in the initial moments of being told about the accident as it had come so closely on the heels of Karl's sudden and violent departure. There were many details she had chosen to leave out.

She didn't regret that in the least.

But she was still unsure how to undo the hard shell she had erected to protect herself and her unborn son. The question remained; did she want to tear down those protective walls?

They had done their job well. She and Tyler had thrived. All her debts were paid, even their small house was slowly coming into her ownership. She had no intention of going into debt ever again. They would have to put up with their small house because Tina was done with loans, debts, and that sort of stress.

Okay, she thought, maybe she did have an extremist way of looking at things. There was nothing wrong with some debt. She was a successful veterinarian. She could probably bear a little burden of debt. But that was not the point. Tina laughed. Even her thoughts didn't want to stick to this particular topic.

How, when, even why should she make friends? Was Tyler really that hard done by if she didn't do it?

Well, now she had the dare with Angela, Rachel, and Evelyn, so she kind of was obligated to do so. But it didn't have to be real. To fulfill the dare, all she had to do was get to know someone new. How hard could that be?

She had already wasted a few days with procrastination. She only had a week left. Tina wasn't sure if she could manage it. The habit of actively avoiding people had become so ingrained.

Obviously, she hadn't always been like that. Once upon a time she had been an outgoing young girl who had made friends readily. Of course, she had been rather exclusive about her best friends, sticking mainly to her friends she ran track and field with, like Rachel and Angela. But even when she went away to college, she had quickly become friends with her roommate and other classmates. Now that concept felt terribly foreign to her.

Tina allowed her gaze to lift from its concentration on the sand in front of her steps, first staring out over the water but then finally forcing it to scan the beach. She supposed that would be the first step. Eye contact with strangers.

The thing she had told Tyler never to do, she thought with a laugh.

Well, she wasn't a ten-year-old. She had even taken some self-defence classes. Surely, she could manage to make eye-contact with strangers without having to break out into a cold sweat.

A jogger was approaching from a distance. Tina desperately wanted to avert her gaze. It felt almost invasive into the other person's privacy to look at them. But that was her hang up. The jogger smiled at her!

Tina's breath came out of her in a whoosh. She hadn't even realized she had been holding it. This shouldn't have felt like an insurmountable task, but she had done it. She had successfully made eye contact with a random person on the beach.

As a reward, Tina sat down and watched the waves come in for a couple minutes. Maybe it was also a form of recovery rather than a reward. She loved the constancy of the waves. Even at the lowest tide they continue to roll toward shore. Living near the beach was one of the best gifts Tina had ever given herself. When she had gone away to college, she hadn't expected to return to her hometown, but after her internship had left her nearly destitute and debt-riddled, she had almost come home to nurse her wounds. She was glad that she had taken that other job in the clinic in New York, though, before returning here. It hadn't felt quite so much like she was coming home a failure. And the experience she had gained in that large clinic had been sufficient for the people of Cape Avalon to trust her with their pets.

And now she could go to the beach almost whenever she wanted. It was a gift, to be sure.

Tina regained her feet and continued her march along the shore. She would challenge herself to encounter a few more people before she returned to Tyler and Clark.

Another jogger was easier than the previous one and she congratulated herself with a grin that was out of proportion to the accomplishment, she was sure, but she didn't care. For her, it was huge.

There were several other walkers she encountered, and she graduated to greetings. Just a wave and a hello, but it was progress to Tina's mind. But she was starting to feel exhausted by the experiment.

One more try, she thought.

A mother with a couple kids playing in the surf.

"Whatcha making?" Tina asked the little girls so studiously building a sandcastle. Or so Tina thought it might be.

"A princess castle," one of them said without taking her eyes off her task.

"You're doing a great job," Tina complimented with a smile as the mother approached.

"Can I help you?" the mother obviously wasn't thrilled about a stranger talking to her daughters. Surprise and embarrassment flooded Tina's chest. She would have reacted the same way. But she wasn't sure how to bridge the awkward encounter with the mother.

"I was just admiring your daughters' handiwork," Tina explained. "I used to do the same when I was growing up here. My son is unfortunately starting to think he's too old for such fun."

The other mother softened a little, nodding sympathetically. "They don't stay this small for long, do they?"

Tina shook her head and actually felt the prickle of the threat of tears. She wanted to run away. Run back to Tyler and the safety of her hard shell, hard, small life. But Tyler needed more than that from her. And this woman seemed like a safe start. Tina swallowed the lump of tears but was fairly sure they would still show in her watery eyes at least a little when she met the other woman's gaze.

"It's both a miracle and a tragedy in my opinion."

The other mother nodded. "How old is your son?"

"He's ten, going on eleven, or rather, really going on nineteen with how mature he's become."

"Oh, that's both lovely and hard. I can see why you're feeling out of sorts about it."

Tina actually laughed at the other woman's wording. "Definitely out of sorts. I'm thrilled that he's growing up well but wish I could keep him little and all to myself at the same time. Which is borderline crazy, isn't it?"

"Probably," the other woman agreed with a little puff of laughter. "But probably the same psychosis afflicts every mother of young kids."

"How do you cope with it?"

"I bury my head in the sand," the other woman answered immediately with another light chuckle. "By that I mean I don't think about the past or future overmuch and try to enjoy the moments."

Tina sighed. "Yeah, that's not my strength. I'm a natural born worry expert."

"That might be par for the course as well. We mothers sure are a complicated lot, aren't we?"

Tina felt genuine amusement welling within her. She peered at the woman a little more closely. She looked to be about the same age as Tina.

"Did you grow up around here?"

The woman shook her head. "No, we moved here about five years ago, right before our youngest was born."

"Moving while pregnant is the worst, isn't it?"

"It is," came the immediate agreement. "But we were glad to be settled, or at least at our destination, before she got here. I was able to stay home longer this way. It helped me settle into the new house and the new role of mothering two small children instead of just one. So, while a bit crazy, the timing actually worked out for us."

Envy colored Tina's reaction for a moment. What would it have been like for her if she had the luxury of a partner who would help her move house and allow her to stay home with her infant for a little longer? Instead, she had been completely alone. Even her parents hadn't been able to join her for Tyler's birth, as it had come on suddenly. And then she had been forced back to finish her schooling and internship immediately. Thankfully, her circumstances were a little better in that she was able to make use of the university child-care arrangement for a short while. But she had been flooded with so many hormones and pain from the birth and had no one to help her cope with it all. Perhaps that had added to her crusty layer. She had done what needed to be done and seemed to have done it well. But not having anyone to help had forced her to erect a wall to keep everyone out even later. Tina shook her head, forcing the thoughts to the back of her mind. They weren't going to help her now.

"So just the two for you, then?" she asked with what she hoped was a pleasant smile.

The other woman nodded. "Two was enough, we thought. Of course, I love the baby stage so much, I would have happily kept having more, but that's not terribly practical, is it?" she asked with a laugh. "How many do you have?"

"Just the one for me. My circumstances changed, and it was no longer a choice."

"Oh?" Curiosity glinted in the other woman's eyes, but she was too polite to inquire further.

Tina's socializing skills were reaching their limit. She had done enough people-ing for the day, in her opinion. She didn't want to put in the intense effort any longer. It was time to take her leave of the pleasant woman and her two adorable children.

"It was nice to meet you today," Tina began as a way to start extracting herself.

The other woman laughed. "We didn't actually meet," she pointed out. "I'm Claire," she added, "and those two rascals are Charlotte and Megan."

"What pretty names," Tina commented. "I'm Tina. My son is Tyler. Maybe we'll see you around the beach again through the summer."

"That would be great," Claire said, but Tina was already turning with a wave and hurrying away. The last expression Tina had noted on Claire's face was one of surprise, but Tina was finished. She had tried and done ok but had overstayed. She should have stopped while she was ahead, before approaching the two girls. She was such an idiot.

She almost stopped in her tracks. She shouldn't speak like that to herself. She wasn't an idiot. Wasn't one of her affirmations that she was smart? And she knew that to be true. Yes, she was a little awkward or even backward socially, but she had actually done not too badly for a first try. She ought to be commending herself, not berating herself. Sure, she could have gone a step further and exchanged phone numbers with the woman or actually made an arrangement to get together with those cute girls and Tyler, but she hadn't. And that was ok. She hadn't insulted the woman. Or been excessively rude. She hadn't even been curt or caustic. She had done well.

Congratulations, Tina, you did well, she thought to herself as she allowed a smile to spread over her face. She had done well. She had approached someone and had a conversation with a polite stranger. She might not have carried it through to enough of a conclusion to count for the dare, but she had at least done the beginning parts. She would have to count it for something. If worse came to worse, she could exaggerate the details ever so slightly and make it fit for the dare, she thought with a laugh as the adrenalin from the experience started to fade and exhaustion threatened to swamp her.

She could only hope there were no animal emergencies that day; she needed a nap.

Her steps were truly lagging by the time she got back to where she had left Tyler and Clark throwing the ball. Tina wasn't even sure how much time had elapsed. She felt like possibly half a millennium but was reasonably sure it couldn't have been that long.

Exhaustion was overwhelming her when she finally slumped onto the blanket she had left in the sand.

"Hey, are you ok?" Clark asked in an overloud voice making Tina wince. Maybe it wasn't that loud, but her senses were reeling.

"Yeah, I'm fine, thanks."

"No, really, Tina, what's wrong?"

"Nothing, Clark. Please just go away. I need a couple minutes." She couldn't even open her eyes to look at him. She hoped Tyler wasn't right there. "If Tyler's ok, could you please just keep him occupied for a few minutes? I'll be ok, I promise."

Tina could feel his stare and wanted to squirm but didn't have the energy. Finally he blew a frustrated breath and stepped away.

Chapter Twenty-One

The emotional rollercoaster was going to make her sick, Tina was certain of it. From the depths of despair to the heights of self-congratulations and back to the bottom of exhaustion. Why was she bothering? Then she heard a squeal from Tyler as he crowed over catching whatever ball Clark had thrown for him, and Tina was reminded of why she was making the effort.

She had to improve at people stuff. Tyler needed her to improve at people stuff. And really, as a functioning human, she would probably benefit from it, too. But she had reached her limit for that day.

Tina rather supposed it was like bike riding. A few months ago, when she had first started trying to get healthier, she had nearly died after that first ride. Now, twelve or thirteen weeks later, she might actually be able to ride all over the whole island with Tyler and barely feel it the next day. Hopefully this would be similar.

She had overexerted herself that day and was feeling the consequences. But if she didn't give up, maybe she might actually get better at it. She could hardly get worse.

She was wrong in that regard and soon found out the truth of it.

Clark wouldn't take no for an answer.

"You aren't ok, Tina, and I need you to tell me why."

"No, you don't, Clark," she said wearily, not even taking her arm away from where it was bent covering her eyes from the glare of the sun.

"Tina, talk to me."

"Please go away, Clark. I'm really trying to be polite here, for the sake of your relationship with Tyler, but you're jumping on my very last nerve."

"I could help."

Finally, Tina erupted, sitting up on the blanket and telling him exactly what she thought of his offer. "You don't have anything to offer me, Clark. You don't even know what my issues are. You are a pretty man who's good at throwing balls. Stick to your lane and leave me to deal with mine. Your relationship is with Tyler, not me. And you're putting even that on the line by insisting on talking to me right now."

Despite the venom dripping from every word she hissed at him, Tina was actually proud of herself that she had managed not to yell or use vile language. Of course, it could probably be argued that it had been vile or at least a little vulgar not to graciously accept his offer of help, but she was well beyond that in the moment.

She shouldn't have threatened to take Tyler away from him, though. That was even lower than low. But he had pushed and pushed until she had felt forced into a corner.

Without another word, Clark turned and walked away. Tina told herself she was glad.

She kept telling herself what a relief it was for days, and then weeks, when the only communication she had with Clark was through text messages when he was making arrangements to spend time with Tyler. Tina was deeply relieved that he was still keeping his position in Tyler's life.

But as she had asked, he was gone from hers. Nothing had ever felt so empty.

Chapter Twenty-Two

"**Y**ou're quiet today, Bud, is everything ok?"

Clark had debated whether or not to ask the question as he was dreading what Tyler might say. The boy wasn't stupid. Surely, he would realize his mentor and his mother weren't really on speaking terms anymore. But it wasn't right to ignore the problem, either. Clark felt strongly that he needed to man up on the matter.

Tyler's sigh sounded melodramatic, but the boy appeared genuinely bothered. Clark steeled himself.

"It's my grampy."

That wasn't what Clark had been expecting.

"What about him?"

"He's sick. Or he might not be. I'm not really sure. My mom said I should try not to worry about it, but I can't help it."

"What makes you think he might be sick?" Clark asked, wondering how he ought to handle the unexpected matter, wishing he was still friendly with Tina as his heart went out to her at the thought of her father being ill.

"We're going into the city this week for an appointment with my grandparents. So, it's something his regular doctor can't deal with. Mom said it's a special doctor for old people, like how little kids have a pediatrist."

Clark had to laugh. "Do you mean a pediatrician?"

"Oh, yeah, I guess so. Do you know what the older people version is called? I forget."

Clark fought against his laughter. "I think it might be a geriatrician. I guess you're right, it is kind of the same."

"Yeah, that's why my mom said I shouldn't worry yet because we don't know what the problem is yet because with that kind of doctor it could be anything. He just specializes in older people."

"So then why are you worrying about it?"

"Well, has anyone ever told you to stop worrying about something? Doesn't that just make it harder to forget about?"

Clark fought back laughter again but couldn't help grinning at the boy as they searched for skipping rocks along the beach by the pier. He had used the excuse that there were better rocks here when he told Tyler where they were going, but really it was just so he wouldn't think about seeing Tina at their favorite beach. He wasn't doing so great with his resolve not to think about her so much. Clark dragged his focus back to the boy at his side.

"I can see your point. How long have you known about it? Have you been worrying the whole time?"

"No," Tyler admitted, sounding mournful. "I can't remember how long I've known, but it was before school ended, I'm pretty sure. But now that we've made the arrangements to go to the city, I can't stop worrying. What if he's going to die?" The last question came out strangled sounding, as though Tyler were trying very hard not to cry.

Clark put all his own cares aside and reached out to put his arm around the boy.

"I'm sorry that you're worrying about this, and I can completely understand why you would find it hard to put it out of your mind. But I can see your Mom's point too that you don't really know what to worry about until after the appointment. Does your Mom seem worried?"

Tyler shrugged. "I think she might be trying to keep it from me. I thought that might be why she hasn't been doing things with us anymore, you know? Maybe so she can help my grandparents."

Clark stifled his sigh. He wished fervently that Tina had given the boy an explanation. He certainly didn't have one for Tyler. Clark wasn't really sure himself what had happened to come between them. But he couldn't tell Tyler that.

"I think your mom just thought it would be better for you and me to spend some time one-on-one together, that's all. I don't think it has anything to do with your Grampy." Although after he said that he wondered if she might have just had too much on her mind and that had caused her blow up. But Clark had no interest in taking the chance on having his head bitten off by her again. He wouldn't ask her until she was ready to speak to him herself.

"So, you're all going to the city with your grandfather, then, is that what you're saying?"

"Yeah," Tyler answered, scuffing his foot into the sand. "Mom said they used to go from time to time when she was my age and they all decided to make it a vacation instead of just to drive in for his appointment."

"Well that sounds like it will be fun, doesn't it?"

"But what if it's like my grandfather's dying wish or something?"

Clark wasn't amused anymore. The poor kid sounded really distressed. "Does your Mom know you're this worried?"

"No, I don't think so. She said we're going to have a good time. I think she might be excited about it. But she doesn't know what it's like not to have a dad."

Clark's heart sank. He knew what it was like.

"Listen, Tyler, I think you should tell your Mom what you've been worrying about, but really and truly, I know for sure the situation with your Gramps is very different than what happened with your Dad. Your father was in a car crash, wasn't he?" At the boy's frowning nod, Clark continued, "The fact that your grandfather is seeing a specialist might mean there's a problem of some sort ,but it also means that he's getting on top of it. There are specialists for this very reason. Doctors can fix so many problems these days. It's possible he's just trying to get ahead of any problems just like your mom is doing with her health."

"What do you mean?"

"Well, you know how your mom is trying to get more exercise and eat more vegetables because she had some warnings from her doctor?"

Tyler nodded. "Yeah, that's why we eat grapes instead of ice cream and carrots instead of chips."

"Exactly. So maybe your grandfather is just seeing this specialist to make sure there aren't any preventable problems in his future, too."

Clark could almost see the wheels turning in the boy's head. "Maybe you could come with us to the city, Clark," Tyler said eagerly. "That would make it even more fun. You haven't even met Grammy and Grampy yet."

Clark swallowed the lump in his throat and forced a laugh.

"I think this might just be an exclusively family excursion for you guys this time."

Tyler's scrutiny made Clark want to squirm. He was only glad the boy didn't ask him any more questions about his relationship with Tina. And it had been weeks since Tyler had asked him about marrying his mom. Thankfully he seemed to have forgotten that idea.

"I'm sure you'll have lots of fun in the city with your mom and grandparents."

Tyler shrugged. "Maybe, but it will probably mean I won't see you for a while."

"We'll survive, but yeah, I'll miss you too."

That seemed to be the final reassurance the youngster was looking for as he happily scampered off to find more stones. Clark sighed, sounding like Tyler had at the beginning of the conversation. Should he tell Tina about the conversation? It wasn't as though they were really sharing confidences these days.

~~~~

"We have to get back in the car now, Tyler."

"But I can't see Clark," Tyler whined, sounding cranky from the late nights in the hotel and the long drive that day.

Tina bit her lip wondering if she ought to warn Clark. She already had in a way. She had been surprised to receive his text message when they were in the city.

Which crossing are you taking to come home? Would Tyler have time to grab a hotdog with me? Or should I just wait to see him next week?

He'd love to see you but it has been a long couple days. He might be tired.

Tina was grateful that Clark was being so kind to her son after her own unkindness toward the man, she didn't want to discourage their getting together, but she wasn't sure how successful their visit would be under the circumstances.

If he's willing, so am I.

And so here they were, on the ferry, hearing the warning about returning to their cars for the final docking and Tyler was too wound up to go below. Tina couldn't blame him. She felt pretty wound up herself. It had turned out that it was a balance issue her father's doctor had been concerned about when he'd referred him to the geriatrician. But the specialist didn't think it was a terribly serious matter. Who knew a build-up of ear wax could make you dizzy? They had all been filled with so much relief they had probably overdone it in the city. And now Tyler was hopped up on too much sugar and not enough sleep.

But Tina trusted Clark could handle it. If only she could entrust herself to him the way her son did. Tina shoved the silly thought from her head. After her behavior, she doubted the handsome man cared for her friendship anyway.

Chapter Twenty-Three

Tina had been right about her supposition that peopling would be like getting physically fit. It did get easier the more she tried it. She still didn't enjoy it immensely, though. And there was now a Clark-sized hole in her life.

Tina recognized the other woman immediately, but her inborn reticence caused her to hold back. Tyler never approached strangers, not even other children, knowing how his mother felt about them. But Tina was trying to turn over all the new leaves.

"It's Claire, right? And Megan and Charlotte?" she asked, walking closer and trying not to allow herself to tighten up. Tyler looked at her with surprise and eagerness evident on his face before he scampered toward the little girls.

Tina was amused despite her discomfort. Children always enjoyed other children.

"Tina, what a pleasure to see you! I was just wishing we had come with friends today and here you turn up. Are you just arriving? Want to join us? This must be your son you were so proud to talk about."

Tina smiled slightly and nodded, fighting her reluctance to decline the invitation. She had asked for it. She needed to follow through. Putting her bag down she offered Claire a more sincere smile. "Thanks, we'd be happy to join you. And yes, that handsome young fella is my son, Tyler." At the mention of his name, Tyler turned and waved.

"Hi, Tyler, this is Charlotte and Megan. They'd love to play with you if you don't mind making sandcastles. That's their obsession right now, and they don't have much mind for anything else."

"I haven't built a great sandcastle in a long time, so I'd love to help," Tyler answered promptly, immediately causing a surge of pride in his mother's heart. He was obviously at least a couple years older than the little girls, but he wasn't too proud to play with them.

"He seems sweet," Claire commented.

"He is," Tina answered immediately. "I'm not sure where he gets it from," she added with a laugh. "I'm not sweet at all, and his father died before he was born."

"Oh no," Claire immediately answered awkwardly, making Tina cringe. Clearly, she needed practice in being with people.

"What are you reading?" Tina asked, turning the subject quickly.

Claire appeared relieved and started prattling about the latest bestseller everyone was talking about. Thankfully she was actually a decent storyteller, so Tina was able to listen with equanimity.

"Sounds interesting, I'll have to look for it."

"Oh, I can give you my copy when I'm done. I never reread a book, and my husband would be thrilled if he didn't have to build any more shelves."

Tina didn't bother protesting, unsure if they would be seeing one another again. But much to her surprise, the afternoon was almost delightful. Probably a normal woman would have been thrilled with her new acquaintance. Tina, on the other hand, kept second guessing everything she did or said, but Claire was remarkably easy going and comfortable to be around. Somehow, she reminded Tina of Clark. But then, everything reminded Tina of Clark these days, ever since she had shoved him unceremoniously out of her life.

But she wasn't going to think about that today.

Claire was reluctant but resolute in leaving at the appointed time. The girls protested, but Claire reminded them that daddy would be home soon and they needed to have supper ready when he got there. That prompted a flurry of activity as the children gathered their things and said goodbye to Tyler.

"Could I get your number?" Claire asked. "Charlotte and Megan have never had a boy be so kind to them, and it's obvious they enjoyed Tyler's company. And I love making mom friends. We should do this again."

Tina ignored the impulse to say no. She wanted mom friends, too. That had been the whole point of her exercise. And after all the effort she and Tyler had gone through to get him a big brother figure, she couldn't turn around and deny Tyler the opportunity to play that same role, albeit very differently than Clark did.

Before she knew how it had happened, she found herself with friendly acquaintances as Angela called them. More than she ever would have expected. All were other moms, either friends of Claire's or the moms of some of Tyler's classmates.

After she gave Claire her number, she followed Evelyn's suggestion of finding the class list and calling the mothers of some of Tyler's particular friends in order to arrange time to spend together.

Which was how she found herself feeling extremely awkward at a barbecue where Clark also happened to be an invitee.

"Fancy meeting you here," Tina had greeted him with a tight smile. She could hear how tight her tone was, but she was highly embarrassed about the last time they had spoken. It had been weeks since they'd actually exchanged words out loud, confining all their communication to text messages since the day she had told him off when she had first met Claire.

"I wouldn't have expected it, either," Clark said, sounding agreeable but distant. "I guess Tyler didn't know you were coming here when I saw him last."

"No, he's still getting used to us having a social life," Tina agreed, looking away feeling all the more uncomfortable with how she had allowed that life to develop without Clark, despite his obvious importance in Tyler's circumstances.

Guilt nearly consumed Tina as she thought about it, besides all the other emotions crowding through her. She needed to do something about it. Keeping herself walled off from feelings had been useful for some things she thought ruefully, but not this.

~~~~

The girls' night had been postponed a couple weeks, which was good. It had allowed time for Tina to come to terms with her own altered reality in order to not bare it all to her friends. She also was able to have a real encounter with someone that wasn't colored by her blow up at Clark.

"All right, all right, ladies," Evie called to quiet the chatter. There was a surprising amount of chatter and noise for only four women in the room. "We still haven't reported on how we did with the challenge. Should we make Tina go first or last, given that it's her fault we did it in the first place?"

209

There was good-natured chatter over that, but Tina was squirming inside. She did not want a spotlight shone on her. What her friends would see was not good. She knew it probably wouldn't be a great surprise to them that she wasn't the nicest person they'd ever met. But she still didn't want to air it out like laundry.

That thought made her chuckle. One could argue that she had been airing it out for years. And it was filthy. It was only now that she was starting to clean it. She was doing her best to turn the snark down to a minimum. But she had done damage in the meantime, and she wasn't sure what to do about that.

Ought she ask her friends for help or suggestions?

If she did, they were likely to think she was "interested" in Clark. She wasn't, of course, she just felt badly about how she had treated him. He had been nothing but good and kind to both Tyler and her. And even in that moment when she'd nearly torn a strip off him, it was because he was trying to be kind to her. His concern had driven her mental.

Or rather, it was his insistence on expressing that concern. Maybe it was even just the way he had worded it. Like he was trying to make her tell him. For the split of a second, it had reminded her of Karl, and everything within her had rebelled. And she had lashed out, damaging a friendship that she hadn't even realized had come to mean so much to her.

She missed the big lug.

Who'd have thought? And it turned out, in hindsight, she realized he wasn't such a neanderthal after all. In the wake of his defection, she realized they had often discussed literature, philosophy, news topics, all sorts of interesting debatable subjects that had nothing to do with sports or whatever meathead men discussed amongst themselves. Despite his appearance, Clark was more of an intellectual than anything else.

An intellectual who could throw a good spiral for Tyler. And fish and camp and all the rest. So basically, he was the perfect guy. But she didn't want to think that. And she couldn't tell her friends about the issue without them thinking she thought that. Which she didn't.

Tina sighed. But she did.

Could she get through the evening without blurting it all out to her friends? She had never been a blurter. But she was all sorts of things she had never been.

"I'm happy to go first or last, whichever makes no difference to me," Tina quickly interrupted her own disquieting thoughts to tell the chattering women, bringing laughter all around.

"You've spoiled our fun, then," Evie said without rancour. "Very well, let's take a vote, did everyone manage to make one new acquaintance?"

Everyone but Angela raised their hand, making the others laugh again.

"Really, Ang?" Rachel exclaimed. "You were the one I expected to have the easiest time of this."

"Perhaps that's because I already know everyone, so I couldn't find anyone new to meet."

"Hmm, that doesn't sound right. Sounds to me like you copped out of the exercise," Rachel complained with a laugh.

"That means the wine is on her for next girls' night," Tina declared making everyone, including Angela, laugh and applaud.

"Fine, fine, I'm the challenge loser, I'll happily pay the forfeit," Angela acknowledged. "But I'll admit to being surprised and impressed that I'm the only one. Can't wait to hear what everyone else has to say."

"I can't wait. I have to say mine," Evelyn interrupted. "I met several people. And one of them is my new social worker who came to inspect our home for our effort to become foster parents."

"Oh, Evie, that's wonderful," Rachel exclaimed.

Tina made all the appropriate noises, she was fairly sure, but she was pretty sure she could never top that with any of her stories. Nor would she want to. It was well known among their friend group that Evelyn was desperate to become a mother. Tina ought to be paying attention to the details Evelyn was sharing, but she was a little too wrapped up in her own misery to join in on the woman's immense joy.

Evelyn was getting her deepest wish. That was absolutely wonderful. And truly, Tina was happy for her. But she was just realizing that she had some deepest wishes that she had never acknowledged to herself or anyone, and she was making herself miserable in the meantime.

After the hubbub died down over Evelyn's announcement, Rachel told a small story about befriending another author who was looking for a critique partner. It was obvious that Rachel too thought any story was going to fall flat after Evie's news. Then all eyes were on her.

Tina sighed. "Yeah, I did the challenge, and I was successful. I met another mom with two little girls and then we actually met up on the beach one day when I was with Tyler, and he played really nicely with her daughters and had a good time. Then Claire introduced me to some other moms and parents, and we've done a few things as groups here and there with the kids."

"Don't sound so enthusiastic, Tina," Rachel said drily. "We'd almost think you were having fun or something."

Tina sighed again and hung her head with a shake. "The problem is, my conscience is bothering me, and I don't know what to do about it."

"Your conscience?" Angela asked. "What have you done?"

Tina laughed despite her disquiet. "Well, I don't know what else to call it. I was inexcusably rude to Clark, and now we aren't friends anymore, so it makes my other new acquaintance-friends feel like a waste of time."

As she had expected, this created a reaction from the other three women, who all stared at her silently for a moment before they all began speaking at once.

"Oh, dear, hun, I'm so sorry," was the most sympathetic, coming from Evelyn.

"That doesn't make it a waste of time," was Rachel's first reaction.

"You LIKE him," Angela squealed with delighted glee making a very brief silence fall over them once more before everyone burst into giggles, even Tina. It couldn't be helped, despite her disquiet.

"You like Clark?" Rachel demanded. "I've only been back on the Cape for a year or so, but I've never known you to crush on anyone. I thought you must have buried your heart with your husband."

"Hush, Rachel," Evelyn said. "I don't think it's like that."

Tina appreciated and yet dreaded the woman's perception.

Angela sobered quickly, realizing the likely veracity of Evelyn's words. "Sorry, Tina, I was just joking around. I shouldn't have said that, sounding like a teenager again."

"Well, I've been feeling like an awkward teenager trying to make friends, so I suppose it's fine." Tina tried to gloss over the moment, regretting allowing it out of the box.

"So, what happened with Clark? How were you rude to him? And has he dropped Tyler along with you?"

"No, he's been a real gentleman with Tyler, not missing a single beat with him. And at first Tyler didn't even notice. But a couple times just lately they've done things that Tyler knows I would like, and he's tried to get me to come along, but since Clark hasn't invited me, I've made excuses."

Rachel reacted as though she supported Tina's way of handling it, but Evelyn and Angela both shook their heads.

"Hun, if you feel bad, you can't just leave it," Evelyn said in a gentle voice.

Angela didn't gloss it over either. "You have to be the change, Tina."

Tina laughed. "You sound even more like Rachel than Rachel does these days, Ange."

"But she would be right in this case," Angela countered. "If you were the rude one, you basically kicked Clark out of your life, right? You might not have meant to do that, but that's basically what happened. So, it's on you to fix it. If you're hoping it will miraculously fix itself or that Clark will take the initiative, you might be waiting a very long time."

"Wait, though, maybe Tina isn't in the wrong," Evelyn pointed out. "Tina, you didn't tell us the circumstances, just that you were rude. Were you really? I know you've been changing a lot lately, were you just your old normal? Or was it something extra?"

Tina sighed. "It was probably pretty extra, even for me. He was actually probably trying to be kind to me, and I told him off for his troubles."

"Why did you do that? Do you know? Or were you just feeling grumpy?" Angela tried to help her get to the bottom of it.

Tina sighed. "Yeah, I know why."

This silenced the other women and brought their curious gazes to rest silently upon her. Finally, Angela gestured as though for Tina to continue, making them all laugh lightly again.

Again, Tina sighed, reluctant to bare her soul to the others despite their close friendship.

"He said something that for the split of a second made him remind me of my late husband."

"Aww and it broke your heart all over again?" Rachel sympathized quickly, but Tina shook her head.

"No, it made me revolt," Tina stated baldly.

"Your marriage wasn't the delight you try to portray it as, was it?" Angela asked gently.

Tears threatened behind Tina's eyes, but she quickly blinked them away even as she shook her head. "But you can't ever tell Tyler," she said immediately and vehemently despite her admitting some of the situation.

"Of course not," Angela replied instantly while the other two just shook their heads with Rachel miming turning a key on her lips.

Tina's sigh felt as though it were coming from her toes. "I won't bore you with the details, but no, Karl and I weren't as happy as we had expected to be. Now, with the passage of time, and listening to Angela talk psychology for years, I realize that Karl was probably struggling with depression or perhaps he had been abused himself, but yes, he was abusive to me. Mostly verbally, but he did hit me on occasion. Not often and only once really badly. But it was enough to mess with my young psyche."

"Of course, it did, you poor thing. I can't believe you never told me. Although there were a few times that I suspected through the years. When you've hated on men or marriage."

Tina lifted her shoulder in a half shrug. "Sorry, Ange. I just didn't want to risk Tyler ever finding out. It's hard enough for him being without a dad. I'd rather him think his dad was awesome. And he was originally. I don't know what happened to him. I was too young, too busy, too wrapped up in my own stresses to think very deeply about what was behind Karl's behavior at the time. I merely reacted in the moment. And built up all sorts of walls and defenses. And then I kept those walls up. For years. I've only started to even think about lowering them in very recent times." She looked around at her three friends. "And I have you to thank for feeling safe enough to even consider it."

There was the sound of murmurs of assent all around as the others accepted her words but awaited further information. Tina let out a puff of frustrated air.

"So back to my Clark situation. There I was, trying to reach out and feel like a normal person interacting with others. We had the dare or challenge or whatever – to make a new acquaintance. So that day I went with Tyler to meet with Clark at the beach just to get out of the house. You remember how restless I was at the beginning of the summer, never having had time on my hands before as an adult. So, while Clark and Tyler played catch or something, I set out to meet people. I remember feeling so awkward about it, I didn't even want to make eye contact with people. But then I started there. Baby steps," she said with a little laugh.

"Then I graduated to nods, then waves or hellos. Then there were these adorable little girls making a sandcastle right in my path, so I stopped to admire their work. Rightly, their mother, Claire, came running over to check on the situation and we actually kind of hit it off. Since then, we've even spent some time together and I've met a bunch of her mom friends. It has been good for Tyler, so I can't say I regret the day. But that day, I came to the end of my strength and rather abruptly ended my conversation with Claire. Anyway, I wandered back to Clark and Tyler feeling like I'd been run over by a truck. Which really is pretty stupid, but that's how I felt. I must have looked it too because Clark was worried and wanted me to tell him what was wrong. Now looking back, I can't even remember exactly what he said but somehow, he triggered an old memory of Karl saying something similar. I will never allow myself to be in that position again, so I lashed out and told Clark to leave me alone. So, he has ever since."

Tina again felt as though she had been run over, but it wasn't the same sensation as the last time. There was a sort of catharsis in finally letting her friends into at least part of her truth. It felt genuine and right even if the telling had exhausted Tina. She waited to hear what the ladies would have to say.

"Oh, hun, I'm so sorry. That was quite an understandable reaction from your point of view and in a certain way you have nothing to feel sorry for. But there is no way that Clark could have known any of that, and he probably just thinks you hate him." Evelyn said it with such kind sympathy, but it still made Tina want to throw up. She hated the thought of having hurt the man.

Angela clasped her hand. "If Clark hasn't abandoned Tyler, what about it bothers you the most? Is it just that you're doing your best to be a better person, so you feel bad that you failed in that moment, or do you want to be friends with Clark?"

"Or more than friends?" Rachel added gently, not sounding like she was seeking salacious gossip.

217

Tina laughed even though she felt a little bit like weeping. "That's just it. I don't really know."

"I think you do, or it wouldn't be eating at you weeks later."

Angela's last comment reached right to the heart of the matter. And was exactly why Tina hadn't wanted to bring it up. She was right. Tina wouldn't be so bothered if she didn't care so deeply.

"So, what do I do?"

"You're going to have to talk to him."

"But he's in a relationship with Tyler," Tina pointed out. "It's really important to Tyler. I would never want to mess with that."

"Seems to me you already tried to, and it didn't take. So, talking to him couldn't possibly make it worse, could it?"

Silence filled the room as Tina reflected on Clark's loyalty to Tyler.

After her outburst, he had taken her at her word, as though acknowledging there was no relationship between them. He was formally polite if they ever did encounter one another, which did happen a time or two throughout that summer at various functions – a barbecue at Rachel and Jake's beach house, a pool party at Angela's family's beautiful home – but he kept his distance at all times from Tina.

But he never abandoned Tyler. At first, Tyler didn't even notice there was anything wrong between his two favorite adults. Not until he wanted Tina to come with them to something or other that he and Clark had planned.

"But you aren't even busy, Mom, why won't you come with us? I'm pretty sure it's something you would really like. Isn't the beach your favorite thing? Don't you want to learn to sculpture sand?"

That had sounded pretty neat to Tina, so she was particularly grateful that she had plans of her own that evening and hadn't had to go into much of an explanation with Tyler. But she was afraid he was starting to become suspicious.

"Maybe I could just ignore the whole thing," Tina began.

"How's that been working for you so far?" Angela asked with a touch of sarcasm. "Isn't that what made you feel so badly that you ended up going against your norm and actually telling us something?"

"I tell you stuff," Tina protested.

"Do you, though?" Angela argued before relenting. "I know you do to a certain extent, but I'm pretty sure there are a few deep, dark secrets you're still keeping. I don't know what they are, but I know you keep them because of Tyler, and so I respect that. But this is obviously bothering you pretty hard or you wouldn't have told us in the least. Because of the connections to those same secrets."

Rachel was nodding along with Angela's words and then interjected, "So that tells us that you need to address it, or it will eat you up. Address it with Clark, I mean. We can help you as much as we can, but it seems the issue is with him."

"Yeah, you're right," Tina agreed. "But for now, let's never mind about that. I'm going to have to think about it some more before I can figure out what I want to do about it. Let's talk about you and Jake, Rachel. Any baby plans on the horizon?"

Tina winced and quickly glanced at Evie to make sure she didn't mind, but that sweet woman waved her concerns away.

"Don't worry, it might not be a baby, but there will be a child filling my nursery soon enough."

The conversation carried on and the evening passed pleasantly, but Tina couldn't get the matter out of her mind.

As she drove home, she thought about the summer she and Tyler had been having and the friendly acquaintanceships she'd been making. She was proud of the changes she had been achieving.

Chapter Twenty-Four

"**H**ello?"

Clark knew full well who was calling him. He had call display on his cell like everyone else. But he hadn't spoken with Tina in weeks. More long, lonely weeks than he wanted to count. He'd missed the wretched woman. He shouldn't. When had he become a glutton for punishment?

He had tried to excuse missing her by the fact that he continued to spend time with Tyler, but Clark was beginning to suspect that wasn't the case. Well, yes, he did spend lots of time with the kid. Great times that both he and Tyler enjoyed immensely. Clark suspected he was spending a lot more time with Tyler than the other Big Brothers spent with their mentees. But Tyler was such a great kid, and it was summertime, so he had plenty of options available for getting together. Clark suspected that would have to come to an end with the school year about to start. That was probably why Tina was calling, as a matter of fact.

But why would she call? All their communication for nearly the entire summer had been via very brief text messages. It was particularly noteworthy how brief they were considering the fact that Tina insisted on spelling every word out instead of using text shorthand.

"Hi Clark, it's Tina Archer calling," she announced with a nervous laugh. "I suppose I didn't need to say my last name. But anyhow. How've you been?"

She sounded incredibly nervous, which conversely put Clark quite at ease. It was unlikely she was calling to terminate his association with her son. If she was going to do that, she would have done it at the beginning of the summer when they'd had their falling out.

"I've been well, thank you, Tina Archer, how've you been?"

"I've been better, I will admit," she said, sounding regretful. "Listen, would you have a few minutes some time where we could maybe grab a coffee or something? I'd rather talk to you in person than on the phone."

"What is this about? Are you going to tell me Tyler's going to soon be too busy to spend time with me?"

There was a brief silence that Clark struggled to understand.

"No, I actually hadn't thought of that. I suppose you two have been spending more time together than he's likely going to have once classes start, but no, that wasn't why I was calling, although I guess we'll have to talk about that, too."

The sigh she heaved made Clark smile despite the tension he was feeling. The prickly woman could always make him smile, except when she was kicking him out of her life.

"I could meet you tomorrow or the next day near your clinic, if that works for you. Depends how much privacy you want, I suppose. We could either grab a table at the coffee shop or take it and walk on the beach."

"Oh, that sounds nice." It almost sounded like wonder in her voice, as though no one had ever made a suggestion to her that they thought she'd like. "Are you sure it's not too much trouble for you? I mean, I could probably come to you if that's better for you."

"Tyler mentioned you were getting busier at your clinic now, so I don't mind. Is tomorrow good? I'd kind of rather get it over with, to be honest." Clark didn't want to be mean or offensive, but he wanted to know what she planned to say, and he didn't think he'd be comfortable waiting.

There was another brief silence where Clark agonized over wondering what she was thinking. If they were in person he would be able to tell, he was sure, so he was glad she wanted to talk in person, he just wished he didn't have to wait.

"I'm sorry, Clark," she finally said, although he wasn't sure what she was apologizing for. "Tomorrow will be good. And I'll try not to take up too much of your time."

He thought there might actually be a sniffle in her voice, but the Tina Archer he knew was hard as nails and never cried, so Clark dismissed the possibility. But it nagged at the back of his mind long after their very brief but stiltedly polite goodbyes. Coffee time the next morning couldn't get there fast enough for him.

Chapter Twenty-Five

I f he wanted to just get it over with, perhaps Tina should have asked him to come over last night, she thought grumpily as she peered into her closet trying to decide what to wear. It was a silly struggle considering she would probably be in a rush and would have to remain in her scrubs. If she had waited a couple of days, she might have been able to meet Clark when Tyler was busy with something, but she wasn't working. But she couldn't wait.

Tyler was going to be busy all day with try outs and practice for the track team. It swelled Tina's heart that he was going for the same team she had done even though he loved ball-type sports so much. He had dismissed her suggestion saying that he could do those things for fun and track and field for the school. He was such a great kid.

She only hoped her conversation with Clark wasn't going to mess up that relationship.

But she was confident in Clark's maturity. If he hadn't cast off Tyler over her previous outburst, he certainly wasn't going to do so when she made an effort to apologize.

She might not make it through the day, though. Nerves were making her entire body tight, and her stomach roil. Time hung heavy on her hands because one of the other parents had offered to drive Tyler to the school. That was one of the great things that had come out of her efforts that summer. While she still didn't count any of them as true friends, she was friendly acquaintances with many of the other parents of Tyler's classmates. It was a nice development that took a little pressure off her and certainly must benefit her son.

How was she going to keep her tension from the animals until it was time to meet up with Clark? That was going to be the big question for the day.

The good thing was, despite the seriousness of some of her cases, it was impossible to be truly uptight with dogs, cats, and bunnies in front of you all day. And so it was that she was able to slick some lip gloss on her lips and tidy up her ponytail but there was no time to even deal with the fur covering her nearly from head to toe if she was going to be on time for their meeting. Her morning had flown by.

"I took the liberty of ordering for you since I was so early, I hope you won't mind," Clark called as soon as he saw her approaching. He looked amazing as usual as he stood tall with the sunshine streaming down onto his head, burnishing his wavy brown hair like gold.

Tina almost rolled her eyes. She must be losing her mind. Now she was becoming poetic in her own mind. How ridiculous. But she managed to control the impulse, just barely. She didn't want him to think she was rolling her eyes at him or his kind gesture of ordering for her. She didn't even care what he had ordered.

"Oh, you didn't have to do that. I actually was planning to treat you," she said, feeling the betrayal of heat climbing into her cheeks. She wasn't sure exactly what she was embarrassed about but there you have it, she was and was feeling super awkward about it. She cleared her throat to rid herself of the clog of nerves.

She gingerly took the cup he was extending toward her, trying not to bush fingers. In her overwrought state she wasn't sure if she was going to throw herself at him or run screaming down the beach, it was best not to tempt herself by any accidental touching at this point.

The way he was anxiously watching her told her he might be just as nervous as she was. "What did you get me? Dark, black coffee or something froofy? You never could decide what I should get, did you?"

Without awaiting his answer, she took a sip and nearly moaned with delight. Her eyes closed to savor the flavor but then she popped them back open. Now was not the time for having a moment.

"What is it? It tastes heavenly!"

Relief spread over his face telling her he had been anxious about her response. She was glad it hadn't been a lie and extra glad she had reacted positively. Without words, they began walking toward the boardwalk.

"I don't really deserve your treating me. Well, I shouldn't even lessen the expression with saying really. I absolutely don't deserve it. I've behaved quite badly and need to apologize. So, you should have waited and made me treat you."

Clark's warm chuckle brought her pleasure that she tried to ignore. She didn't deserve his swift forgiveness, but she should have known he would be kind. It was one of the many things she liked about him.

"It gave me something to do. I should have gone with the black coffee because I almost threw this one out a couple times thinking you might not like it. But never mind about that, why do you say you don't deserve it? Everyone deserves to be treated from time to time."

Tina sighed. "Well, I haven't been on the receiving end of such in a very long time, but that's not my point. Clark—" She stopped in her tracks and turned to him, grateful that the boardwalk was pretty much empty, and they were in a wider section of it anyway so they wouldn't be inconveniencing anyone with her fits and starts. "I was so rude to you that day weeks ago, and I ought to have apologized right away, but I was cowardly and didn't. But I can't stand the coldness between us. Do you think you could possibly accept that I'm terribly sorry and let us be friends again?"

Clark's grin was wide and breathtaking, and the final seal on her lack of breath was when he put his hand on the small of her back and urged her along the railing so they could stand with their drinks and look out at the waves.

"Would you rather walk or talk? I don't think I can do both in this moment," he said, looking down at her with a warm glint in his eye.

"Talk, for sure, please, tell me quick."

Clark chuckled but took a sip of his drink before he looked down at her again. "Of course, I forgive you. I didn't really think there was anything to forgive. I just thought you didn't want to be friends. So, I gave you what you asked for."

"Well, that was daft. I'm an idiot. You shouldn't give an idiot what they ask for," Tina complained.

Clark laughed again but shook his head. "You're definitely not an idiot. And I will happily be friends with you, but I would appreciate a bit of an explanation of what caused the outburst that day, if you didn't mean it the way I took it."

Tina felt the burn of tears at the back of her throat but quickly blinked them away. She wasn't sure if they were caused by relief over his ready willingness to be friends or the memories that swamped her over that day weeks ago or the further past that had caused her outburst.

Tina sighed. "It's a really long story. Are you up for it? Do you need to get back to your job site at a certain time?"

To her surprise, Clark suddenly appeared bashful. "I actually told Jake I wouldn't be back after lunch."

"Oh, I'm sorry, I didn't mean to mess up your day. I didn't intend to take too much of your time."

"Yeah, I figured, but depending on the tone of our conversation, I figured it might be best that I not be around power tools afterward, and I didn't want to leave him in the lurch on even shorter notice."

Tina sighed again. "I have lots to be sorry for, it seems, then."

"No, this isn't on you. My mental state is my choice." He sounded almost as though he were growling at her, but Tina didn't really hate it. She could listen to him all day. She was an idiot. "Now, please, tell me why you hated on me that day."

Tina took a long sip of the sweet caffeine and kept her gaze on the waves, but then she turned to Clark with a wrinkled nose. "Since you won't be the one talking, would you mind if we walk while I spill my guts? It'll help me get it said."

"Of course," Clark replied immediately turning and beginning to stroll, allowing for her shorter stride.

"You can't ever tell Tyler any of what I'm about to tell you. I've kept it my deepest secret for his entire life because I believe it would be damaging to him."

"Your secrets are always safe with me, Tina," Clark vowed, making her melt even further inside and castigate herself even more. The man was a saint. Why had she denied herself his friendship all this time?

"I won't bore you with all the details, but suffice it to say, my marriage was a disaster almost from the very beginning. I've been thinking a lot about it in recent weeks. For years I've placed all the blame on him, but I can see now that the blame for at least the beginnings of the problems could be shared by both of us." Tina sighed and shrugged, feeling a little silly to be telling him this despite her need to explain herself. "I had thought we would live happily ever after, but I don't think either of us were equipped to put in the work required to achieve that. We were very young. And it turns out at least one of us, probably both, were too selfish to give the other what they needed. Karl was far more chauvinistic than I had ever realized. He expected me to be home cooking and cleaning whenever he thought appropriate despite my heavy course load to finish out my degree. It got pretty nasty for a time."

"Did he hit you?" Clark demanded, sounding furious.

"He might have," Tina replied lightly, "but that was far less damaging, in my opinion, than the words he used regularly." She took a deep breath. "And then he blamed me for getting pregnant, as though somehow I had accomplished it on my own." She tried to force a laugh and gloss it over, but it sounded like little more than a squeak. Tina waved her hand in front of her face as though to eliminate the experience. "Anyhow, I've never allowed a man into our lives after that, until you. As you are well aware, it was a big deal for me to let you into Tyler's life. I actually didn't allow almost anyone into our lives, to be honest. So, this summer, seeing how much good you were doing for Tyler, I thought we ought to try to expand our horizons even more, and I made myself be more open to other people. That day was my first try." Tina was so glad she didn't have to look at him fully while she told her sorry tale, as they walked along. It was a grim account for such a glorious day. She carried on despite her reluctance.

"As you might remember, I was already out of sorts when we met with you. You even commented on it, but I dismissed what you were asking thinking I would be fine. Turns out, I was already worked up at the very thought of it. And then I made myself do it. So, when I came back to you and Tyler, I was at the end of my endurance. I could barely see straight; I was so worked up. In hindsight, I realize you were expressing concern. But for a split moment, the way you expressed it, I can't even remember exactly how now, it reminded me of Karl. I think you said something along the lines of insisting I tell you. I freaked out. I had promised myself no one would ever insist on anything with me again. Because of that I put up all these walls around me and Tyler, limitations really. They protected us for a time, but now they have to go. And I was really trying. But it was hard for me. And you got shot down in the crosshairs. I'm truly sorry, Clark. It was totally me, not you. And I'm sorry too that it took me so long to say that I'm sorry."

"Why did it? From what I've heard from Tyler, you have been doing a pretty good job of making friends and being more open with people. Why couldn't you allow me to be a part of that?"

Tina held her breath. This was the moment she had dreaded. She was going to have to truly bare her soul and take a risk with her heart. But she was strong enough now. She didn't need the walls. Even if Clark didn't want anything more than a polite friendship, that was going to be perfectly all right. She had her friends, she had her friendly acquaintances, and most of all, she had Tyler. She would be just fine. But she could be better than fine. So, she was going to risk it. She let her breath out slowly.

I am healthy. I am wealthy. I am pretty. I am kind. The remembered affirmation made her smile and helped her get over the flutter of fear.

"Because you are a much bigger deal than the parents of classmates or random strangers I've met at the beach. You're very important to Tyler, for one thing."

Clark frowned and interrupted her. "Are you jealous of that?"

"No, of course not," Tina countered. "But I'm a little afraid that a mess between you and me would cause a rift between you and him."

"I'm reasonably sure it has been proven that isn't the case."

"Yeah," Tina drawled. "I've noticed. And I've so appreciated that, Clark, you have no idea."

"So, what's the problem?" Clark was confused.

Tina blew out the breath she had been holding. "My friends had to help me to understand it, actually. I didn't realize that my problem was not that I didn't like you, but rather I liked you too much. I haven't "liked" a boy since Karl, you see."

Clark blinked and stared at her while a wide grin slowly spread across his face. "You like me? As in like me like me?" he asked with a deep chuckle even as his hand returned to the small of her back sending chills and tingles throughout her limbs and setting off the flutter of butterflies in her midsection. "I thought I'd never have a chance with you."

Tina stopped dead in her tracks and stared up at him, feeling suddenly small and dainty and fluttering with nerves. "What do you mean?"

"Well, I liked you from the beginning."

"Really?" she asked drily. "From the wedding?"

"Well, I thought you were pretty right from the beginning. I did think you were a bit crusty until I got to know you better. But I've liked you quite immensely for ages."

"Even after I told you to shove off."

"Yeah, that was disappointing to say the least," Clark admitted. "I tried to put you out of my mind, but it's a little difficult when I enjoy spending time with your son so much."

Tina sighed once more. "Well that brings us to the tricky point. You aren't just some random guy. You're Tyler's mentor. I don't want him getting his hopes up about something. Nor do I want him getting hurt."

"Neither of us will ever hurt your son, Tina, I can swear to that. But I do understand about his hopes," Clark said slowly. "On the other hand, I feel like we have gotten to know each other pretty well over the last months. Maybe getting all of our hopes up is perfectly okay."

Tina blinked up at him as she felt those very hopes that she meant to keep hold of start to soar. But she needed to lighten the moment with a joke. "You aren't about to propose are you?"

Clark grinned but didn't deny it right away, making Tina's heart flip in all sorts of unnatural ways.

"Maybe not yet," Clark finally said, "But I'd very much like to consider kissing you."

"Are you awaiting permission?" she whispered.

"No, I'm savoring the moment," he replied as his head descended towards hers.

The End

Other books by W. M. Andrews:

Return to Sandpiper Cottage

is the first book in the **Cape Avalon** series.

Return to Sandpiper Cottage and *Shelter at Sugar Beach* are Ms. Andrews' first contemporary set stories. If you're interested in reading her Historical Romance fiction, visit the Book Series page on her website to learn more.

Consider starting her latest series –
Northcott Kinship.

Intriguing Lord Adelaide

She's a wallflower debutante—and his best friend's sister. But one dance could change everything.

About the Author

I learned to read when I was four or five, listening to my mother read to me when I was lonely after my brother started school. Ever since, I've had my head buried in books. I love words – historical plaques, signs, the cereal box – but my first love has always been novels.

A little over ten years ago my husband dared me to write a book instead of always reading them. I didn't think I'd be able to do it, but to my surprise I love writing. Those early efforts eventually became my first published book – Tempting the Earl (published by Avalon Books in 2010). It has been a thrilling adventure as I learned to navigate the world of publishing.

I believe firmly that everyone deserves a happily ever after. I want my readers to be able to escape from the everyday for a little while and feel upbeat and refreshed when they get to the end of my books.

When not reading or writing, I can be found traipsing around my neighbourhood or travelling the world with my favourite companion.

Stay in touch with Wendy May Andrews
and her upcoming publishing news.

Sign up for her biweekly newsletter at
wendymayandrews.com

Made in the USA
Las Vegas, NV
03 January 2024

83870359R00142